TW
NEW ZEALAND
CHILDREN'S
WRITERS

To Huia,

Welcome home;

May you find

aroha

everywhere you go.

Thankyou for the
opportunity to share
your world —

May God richly bless you!

from

Bryan, Ro, Kathy Anna
& Sarah.   Aug. 1991.

For my father with gratitude
and in memory of my mother

INTRODUCING
TWENTY-ONE NEW ZEALAND CHILDREN'S WRITERS

BETTY GILDERDALE

Hodder & Stoughton

AUCKLAND LONDON SYDNEY TORONTO

Photo credits: p. 37 Otago Daily Times; pp. 53, 59 Gil Hanly;
p. 74 Colin Smith; p. 87 Christchurch Press; p. 99 NZ Herald;
p. 125 Taranaki Newspapers.

Typeset by Glenfield Graphics Ltd, Auckland
Printed and bound in Hong Kong for Hodder & Stoughton Ltd,
46 View Road, Glenfield, Auckland, New Zealand.

CONTENTS

PREFACE

Twenty years ago it would have been very difficult to write this book because there simply were not enough New Zealand authors of quality fiction for children to have justified it. Today the situation is reversed, and there are so many able writers of junior fiction that it is difficult to choose between them. Because this book is primarily intended for readers between the ages of eight and thirteen, the writers selected are those writing for that age group. Authors writing exclusively for younger children or for young adults have not been included.

The only two exceptions are Ronda Armitage and Lynley Dodd. Both are Esther Glen Award winners and both are so widely known and loved that any publication on New Zealand writers that failed to include them would seem incomplete. Most young readers will have enjoyed *The Lighthouse Keeper's Lunch* and the Hairy Maclary books at primary school.

I would like to take this opportunity to thank all the authors represented here for their cooperation and to say how much I have enjoyed meeting, talking and corresponding with them. Writers of fiction, it seems, are as varied as any other segment of society. Some talk freely about themselves and their interests, but others prefer their books to speak for them.

Every effort has been made to give complete bibliographies up to and including 1990. The only exception is in books intended as beginner readers and published by educational publishers. The reason for this is that authors such as Margaret Mahy and Joy Cowley have been so prolific that a list of every title would take up numerous pages. Accordingly, the publishers and series have been noted and they can be referred to if required. The size of this particular problem was highlighted by Joy Cowley who, when asked whether she could isolate the starting point of her stories, pointed out that there were more than 200 of them and added, 'You're joking, surely!'

RONDA ARMITAGE

Born   Kaikoura, 11 March 1943. She has two children, and she lives in Sussex, England.

Pets   Cats. Hamish, alas, is no more but she now has Rosie and Rusty.

Favourite food   Everything, but especially crayfish and tropical fruits such as feijoas and mangoes.

Favourite pastimes   Reading, gardening and travel.

Favourite authors   Children's: Philippa Pearce, Rosemary Sutcliff. Adults': Robertson Davies and Tim Morrison.

Profession   Teacher.

Awards   NZ Library Association Esther Glen Award 1978 for *The Lighthouse Keeper's Lunch*.

One day when Ronda Armitage was walking with her family near Beachy Head in southern England her four-year-old son Joss noticed a cable running from a lighthouse on the rocks to the top of the great white cliffs. 'What's that for?' he asked. His father, artist David Armitage, did not really know, but jokingly guessed, 'Perhaps it's for the lighthouse keeper's lunch!' This was the beginning of what was to become one of the world's best-loved picture books. *The Lighthouse Keeper's Lunch* won the Esther Glen Award and is now among the 100 most-borrowed books in British libraries.

The lighthouse keeper and his wife, Mr and Mrs Grinling,

not to mention their cat Hamish, have now appeared in three books. In the first Mrs Grinling solves the problem of how to stop seagulls from eating Mr Grinling's lunch as it travels in its basket along the wire. The Armitages found the starting point for the second story when David Armitage was locked out of the house. They wondered what would happen if Mr Grinling were locked out of the lighthouse, with Hamish and the key locked *inside*. The result was *The Lighthouse Keeper's Catastrophe*, in which Hamish is a central character.

In the third book Mr Grinling loses his job. Lighthouses no longer have keepers — a fact that greatly saddens the Armitages. They had once thought of applying to be lighthouse keepers. The idea of living on some remote stretch of coast appealed to them.

Ronda had become used to living in out-of-the-way places when her parents farmed in remote country between Rotorua and Whakatane. She went to a small school where she was one of only three pupils in her class. They were four kilometres away from the nearest family and her sister was nearly five years younger than she was. This left her plenty of time for reading. She loved family stories like *Little Women, Anne of Green Gables* and *What Katy Did*, but she also enjoyed the really stirring tales such as *King Solomon's Mines* and the stories of G. A. Henty.

Ronda Armitage does not remember doing any story writing at school, but she does remember that when she was ten years old she and a visiting cousin spent a whole summer holiday writing. They put a very imposing notice on the door saying, 'Authors at Work — DO NOT DISTURB!' When she was a boarder at St Cuthbert's in Auckland, Ronda found being constantly surrounded by people very trying. She found time to read but not to write.

She first became interested in children's books when she trained as a teacher and discovered how important it is to read to children. Later on, after marrying artist David Armitage, she worked in Dorothy Butler's world-famous children's bookshop in Auckland, until Joss was born. He was followed by a daughter, Kate, and the family moved to Sussex in England, where they still live. They never did get to their lighthouse!

The children, Joss and Kate, have often been the inspiration in their books. In *The Bossing of Josie*, renamed *The Birthday Spell*, Josie, like Kate, has been given a witch's costume. Like Matilda, the small bear in *Don't Forget Matilda*, Kate was inclined to be forgetful. Joss, deciding to camp out for the night, triggered off the adventures of *One Moonlit Night*.

Getting an idea is one thing, but working on it and expanding it into a well-shaped story is another. The Armitage books often start with a problem and the rest of the tale shows how it is solved. After all, Ronda Armitage says, 'I spend my own life solving problems.'

A careful look at their picture books shows how well Ronda, the writer, cooperates with David, the artist. Ronda gives David only the bare bones of the story. Although she sees all the details in her mind's eye, she leaves them to David to put in the pictures. Her great gift as a writer is in choosing exactly the right word. She never simplifies her language because she is writing for younger children. Mr Grinling is 'conscientious', Mrs Grinling 'concocts delicious lunches', the seagulls are 'scavengers' and Mrs Grinling's plan is 'ingenious'.

Ronda Armitage's love of fun and of interesting language shines through in *Grandma Goes Shopping*, which lists Grandma's strange and unusual purchases. These include an amiable alligator, a variegated vicuna, a tootling flute and a flügel horn.

Grandma gets back in time for tea, and food is very important in all the Armitage books. It is central to *Ice Creams for Rose*, sandwiches are almost forgotten in *Don't Forget Matilda*, there is comforting hot chocolate after the alarms and frights in *One Moonlit Night* and there is a triumphant birthday party at the end of *The Bossing of Josie*.

Joss and Kate are grown up now, but David and Ronda have by no means lost touch with children. They spend at least one day a week working in schools, and in her remaining time Ronda works as a family counsellor. She moved into this from teaching when she became concerned about various social problems she saw. She had taught small children who were sent to school with no breakfast, whose parents never read stories to them, or who had so many troubles at home that they came to school unhappy and unable to concentrate. Amongst teenagers one of the greatest problems is alcohol. She says it is the biggest killer of the young people, who drink and drive. Her non-fiction book, *Let's Discuss Drinking*, gives the facts about alcohol.

But Ronda Armitage's main work as a writer will always be in picture books with David. She is never quite certain where her ideas come from. She says they seem to float into her head, often in the bath late at night. Later she writes them down in longhand, rewriting at least three or four times before typing.

She is not tempted to write longer books for older children. That would be the task of a novelist. She sees herself more as a short-story writer or poet. She says, 'Picture books are for reading aloud, the story must flow smoothly and each sentence needs to be rhythmic. This form of writing is perhaps more akin to poetry than to prose, in the sense that each word has to play its part — after all, there aren't many of them.'

BIBLIOGRAPHY

Books for children

Fiction
All illustrated by David Armitage:
The Lighthouse Keeper's Lunch. André Deutsch, London, 1977.
The Trouble with Mr Harris. André Deutsch, London, 1978.
Don't Forget Matilda. André Deutsch, London, 1979.

The Bossing of Josie. André Deutsch, London, 1980.
    Retitled *The Birthday Spell.* Hippo, London, 1981.
Ice Creams for Rosie. André Deutsch, London, 1981.
One Moonlit Night. André Deutsch, London, 1983.
Grandma Goes Shopping. André Deutsch, London, 1984.
The Lighthouse Keeper's Catastrophe. André Deutsch, London, 1986.
The Lighthouse Keeper's Rescue. André Deutsch, London, 1989.
When Dad Did the Washing. André Deutsch, London, 1990.

Non-fiction
Let's Discuss Drinking. Wayland, Hove, 1987.
Countries of the World: New Zealand. Wayland, Hove, 1988.

RON BACON

Born   Melbourne, Australia, 18 June 1924. He has three grown-up children, several grandchildren and one great-grandchild. He lives in Auckland.

Pets   A budgerigar named Charlie who 'helps' him when he is writing by nibbling his pen, attacking his typewriter and saying, 'Good morning, Charlie!' or 'I'm a turkey!' or even 'Good morning, turkey, I'm a Charlie!'

Favourite food   Chocolate, but he is on a diet and is not allowed very much.

Favourite pastimes   Reading, weaving, woodcarving, painting in acrylics, gardening and walking.

Favourite author   Lynley Dodd. He reads widely among adult authors.

Profession   Before retiring he was principal of Favona School, Auckland.

Awards   NZ Picture Book of the Year 1984 for *The Fish of our Fathers.*

Ron Bacon was a lonely child. He had no brothers or sisters until he was eight, when his sister was born. He and his parents moved to New Zealand from Melbourne when he was six years old and so there were no cousins, aunts, uncles or grandparents to visit them. He had no one to play with at home, and no toys except for an old rag doll called Redwing.

But being alone did not mean being bored. In the days before television he learned to love being out-of-doors and soon knew where every bird had its nest. It was the beginning of a life-long interest in nature, which is reflected in the titles of some of his books, such as *Wind* and *The Bay*. Very recently he has written a non-fiction book, *Save Our Earth*, which he says may well be the most important thing he has ever written. In *Save Our Earth* he points out the dangers of the Greenhouse Effect and the hole in the ozone layer, and he hopes that everyone who reads it will follow his suggestions for saving our planet.

Ron's parents may not have given him toys, but his mother gave him something much more valuable. She loved books and was herself a marvellous teller of tales, so Ron Bacon grew up with stories. When he was not listening to them he was making up his own, and when he was only seven years old one of them, 'Spring Song of Birds', was published in the *Evening Post*.

By the time he left school, where he was always good at English and art, the Second World War had begun. At the age of eighteen he found himself in the Royal New Zealand Air Force as a ground-crew armourer, and he served in the Pacific area until the end of the war. When he came back to New Zealand he drifted into teaching and trained at Ardmore Teachers' College, near Auckland. He says that if he had to choose a career now he would become an artist. He would love to be able to illustrate his own books, but he has very high standards and prefers to work with professional artists.

Teaching may not have been his first choice, but he did enjoy being with children and especially enjoyed taking lessons in language and art. At first he worked in small country schools in the North Island, and he wrote about his experiences in a book for adults called *In the Sticks*. It was through teaching that he discovered how few stories about New Zealand's past there were for children, and how very few there were about

Maori subjects. As a result his two books *The Boy and the Taniwha* and *Rua and the Sea People* were landmarks in New Zealand children's literature. *The Boy and the Taniwha* tells how a Maori boy lives with his grandmother, who shares her wisdom with him, until he finds a taniwha and passes his test of manhood. *Rua and the Sea People* describes how Rua first sees white men when Captain Cook lands.

The two books were unusual not only in subject matter but also in illustration, because Ron Bacon insisted that the pictures should be done by a Maori artist. He chose Para Matchitt and the result is beautiful designs in which Maori traditional patterns are used.

His next book, *Again the Bugles Blow,* was for older readers and was one of New Zealand's first 'time-slip' novels. A twentieth-century boy — another Rua — falls and hits his head and while he is unconscious he goes back in time to see the tragic battle of Orakau, in which his ancestors had fought. It is an exciting story but a sad one: there were good people on both sides but they were caught up in events beyond their control.

By now Ron Bacon was married and had three children — two sons and a daughter. He was increasingly busy at school and there seemed to be too little time to write novels. But stories sang themselves into his head and he concentrated on writing them down so that they would sound as natural and absorbing as a tale told by firelight on a winter's night.

He had become very interested in Maori legends and collected many different versions of the stories. But just writing the plot of a story is not at all the same thing as making it vivid. The man who wanted to paint had to become an artist with words. In 'The Land Under the Earth' he has really imagined the scene:

The ghost people under the earth were skinny and grey. They had long bony arms and eyes of fire...The land, too, was grey. There were no green trees, only grey ghost trees. There was no green grass, only grey ghost grass. There was no blue sky over the land under the earth. There was only a grey sky made out of the earth of the land above. No light from the sun came through the grey earth sky, only the grey roots of trees.

We have been helped to enter into that scene with what looks to be very simple writing. Unfortunately for authors, what is easy to read is often the result of a great deal of hard work. When Ron Bacon is retelling a story he starts in one of the big diaries he buys cheaply at half-yearly sales, and he may work and rework one sentence as many as twenty times until it sounds just right. He then reads it aloud on to audio tape, so that he can check whether the language is rhythmical, before he types the final copy.

In 1984 he was given the New Zealand Picture Book of the Year Award for *The Fish of our Fathers*. This is one of a series of three most unusual books, the first of which, *The House of the People*, tells how the first Maori meeting-house was built and explains the symbols in the decorations on carvings and wall panels. *The Fish of our Fathers* shows the building of the first war canoe and in *Home of the Winds* the story is about the first pa. All three are strikingly illustrated by Maori artist R. F. Jahnke, who has used the traditional earth colours and patterns of Maori design.

It comes as a surprise to find that Ron Bacon never read his own stories to the classes he taught. He is basically a shy person and did not want to force his work on the children he knew. He is retired from teaching now, but is invited to schools so frequently that he finds he has less time than he had expected to pursue his hobbies of woodcarving and weaving. He has to be very firm even to get enough time for writing.

Recently he has turned to non-fiction. His clear style makes for easy understanding in books such as *Weaving, Publishing a Book* and *Let's Make Music*.

Now that he has more time he is once again creating his own themes rather than retelling legends. All his beliefs about the importance of stories and of art seem to have come together in *The Clay Boy*, in which a boy who longs to paint cannot find the right materials and receives no encouragement from his tribe. After much searching he finds the clays he needs to make glowing colour and produces such fine paintings that his tribe is proud of him. If 'paintings' were changed to 'words', this could almost be the story of Ron Bacon himself.

BIBLIOGRAPHY

Books for children

Fiction

The Boy and the Taniwha. Illus. Para Matchitt. Collins, Auckland, 1966.

Rua and the Sea People. Illus. Para Matchitt. Collins, Auckland, 1968.

Again the Bugles Blow. Collins, Auckland, 1973. Hodder & Stoughton, Auckland, 1984.

The House of the People. Illus. R. F. Jahnke. Collins, Auckland, 1977.

Hatupatu and the Bird Woman. Illus. R. F. Jahnke. Collins, Auckland, 1979.

The Fish of our Fathers. Illus. R. F. Jahnke. Waiatarua, Auckland, 1984.

The Creation Stories. Illus. R. F. Jahnke. Shortland, Auckland, 1984.

The Maui Stories. Illus. Cliff Whiting. Shortland, Auckland, 1984.

Seven Stories. Illus. Philippa Stichbury. Shortland, Auckland, 1984.

Hemi Dances. Illus. Sharon O'Callaghan. Waiatarua, Auckland, 1985.

Wind. Illus. Philippa Stichbury. Ashton, Auckland, 1985.

Ruru and the Green Fairies. Illus. Frank Bates. Waiatarua, Auckland, 1985.

Hoto Puku. Illus. Frank Bates. Waiatarua, Auckland, 1985.

Little Pukeko and the Tiki. Illus. Frank Bates. Waiatarua, Auckland, 1985.

Maui and Kuri. Illus. Frank Bates. Waiatarua, Auckland, 1985.

The Home of the Winds. Illus. R. F. Jahnke. Waiatarua, Auckland, 1986.

A Legend of Kiwi. Illus. Steve Dickinson. Waiatarua, Auckland, 1987.

The Bay. Illus. Sandra Morris. Ashton Scholastic, Auckland, 1987.

Hemi and the Whale. Illus. Sharon O'Callaghan. Waiatarua, Auckland, 1988.

Waikaremoana. Illus. Steve Dickinson. Waiatarua, Auckland, 1988.

Tangaroa and the Tekoteko. Illus. Steve Dickinson. Waiatarua, Auckland, 1988.

The Fisherman's Tale. Illus. Steve Dickinson. Waiatarua, Auckland, 1988.

The Green Fish of Ngahue. Illus. Mary Taylor. Waiatarua, Auckland, 1989.

Hay for the Donkey. Illus. Steve Dickinson. Waiatarua, Auckland, 1989.

The Clay Boy. Illus. Chris Gaskin. Hodder & Stoughton, Auckland, 1989.

A Mouse Singing in the Reeds. Illus. Mary Taylor. Hodder & Stoughton, Auckland, 1990.

Three Surprises for Hemi. Illus. Anita Vink. Waiatarua, Auckland, 1990 .

The Banjo Man. Illus. Kelvin Hawley. Ashton Scholastic, Auckland, 1990.

Non-fiction

Publishing a Book. Shortland, Auckland, 1987.
Let's Make Music. Shortland, Auckland, 1987.
Games and their Past. Shortland, Auckland, 1987.
Unsolved Mysteries. Shortland, Auckland, 1987.
Code and Messages. Shortland, Auckland, 1987.
Rainy Day Ideas. Shortland, Auckland, 1987.
Save Our Earth. Shortland, Auckland, 1988.
Weaving. Shortland, Auckland, 1988.
The Printing Machine. Shortland, Auckland, 1989.
Masks. Shortland, Auckland, 1990.

8 readers for Shortland, Auckland, 1986–89.

Books for adults

In the Sticks. Collins, Auckland, 1963.
Along the Road. Collins, Auckland, 1964.
Auckland: Gateway to New Zealand. Collins, Auckland, 1968.
Auckland Town and About. Collins, Auckland, 1973.

MARGARET BEAMES

Born   Oxford, England, 18 October 1935. She has two grown-up children and three grandchildren. She lives in Feilding.

Pets   A large, lazy cat called Spider, who is thirteen years old. Until last year, when she died, a German shepherd dog.

Favourite food   She is a vegetarian, so likes fresh natural food. She dislikes fatty food but does like chocolate.

Favourite pastimes   Reading, crossword puzzles, knitting, spinning and patchwork. She loves the theatre, travel and music (except rock), which she plays while she works.

Favourite authors   So many it's hard to say. As a child she liked Kenneth Grahame's *The Wind in the Willows*, Susan Coolidge's Katy books, the Biggles books by Captain W. E. Johns, Richmal Crompton's William books and R. M. Ballantyne's adventure stories. Adults': Jane Austen, Charlotte and Emily Brontë, Doris Lessing, Fay Weldon and Peter Carey.

Likes   Sitting looking at the sea doing nothing.

Dislikes   Loud noise and cruelty to people and animals. She also worries about the pollution of air, sea and soil.

Profession   A teacher in England. She now helps children with specific learning disabilities.

Margaret Beames was the middle child in a family of three, but was often alone because she had asthma and could not join in sport — one reason she enjoyed reading and writing so much. When she first came to New Zealand in 1974 she could not find a teaching job and says she was 'homesick, lonely and bored'. She thought she would see whether she could write a book, and she decided that the best way to begin would be to invent some characters. She knew a great deal about children, her own and other people's, so she invented a family of five children. Then she started wondering what would happen if a family of children were sent to stay with an aunt, but when they arrived she was not there. In *The Greenstone Summer* the children arrive at their aunt's house in the far north of New Zealand to find groceries unpacked on the table, a dog thirsty and starving, and no sign of their aunt. In an exciting story we discover how her disappearance is connected with the theft of some Maori artefacts.

Authors like Margaret Beames, Joan de Hamel and Eve Sutton, who all came to New Zealand from Great Britain, say they wanted to find out more about what happened here in the past. It was a visit to Kelly Tarlton's Shipwreck Museum at Paihia that set Margaret Beames thinking about how many early settler ships must have been driven onto the rocky coast during storms. What would have happened, she wondered, if a farmer had ordered some prize cattle and the ship was blown onto rocks? What if one of the cattle to escape had been a fierce bull?

Her second book, *Hidden Valley*, grew from this idea. It tells how a brother and sister, Vicky and Johnny, who lived at the beginning of this century, hear that a prize bull has escaped from a wrecked ship. The bull has apparently swum ashore, but no one has seen where it has gone. Vicky, Johnny and their friend Carrie discover it deep in a hidden valley, but they are then faced with getting the bull out. Not the least of their difficulties is the fact that Carrie's governess and Vicky's aunt do not approve of girls' being involved in such adventures. The aunt and governess are among some very interesting characters in *Hidden Valley* and, although the book is set nearly a hundred years ago, it is plain that children in those days were not so very different from those who live today.

Vicky and Johnny have a settled way of life at home and at school, but Charlie Blackiston, the hero of Margaret Beames's next novel, has a much less fortunate life. The book had its beginnings when she read an article in the New Zealand *Listener*, about young boys who had been brought out to New Zealand from an English prison in 1842. Margaret Beames was astonished. She knew that convicts had been taken to Australia, but young prisoners in New Zealand? She decided to find out whether it was true and the result of all her research was *The Parkhurst Boys*.

Charlie Blackiston is an orphan who has been sent to a harsh boarding school in England. He runs away because he is so unhappy there, but he has no money and is nearly starving when he is befriended by a young street kid, Joss. They find that the only way they can get food is to steal it, but they are arrested and sent to Parkhurst Boys' Prison. Later they are among the boys to be brought out to New Zealand. The story follows them on the journey and tells how Charlie is apprenticed to an unkind woman and runs away to Great Barrier Island. Meanwhile Joss is also working in Auckland and someone from England is looking for Charlie...

Both Margaret Beames's books about the past are exciting adventure stories, but after the last page is read and the book put back on the shelf you realise how much more you know about the early days of European settlement in New Zealand.

Her latest book, *Clown Magic*, is not about the past, however. It is one of the few New Zealand stories to be set in a present-day city at Christmas time. So many Christmas stories come from the Northern Hemisphere, where there is snow, holly and crisp cold air, that it comes as a surprise to find a book beginning with a family doing their last-minute shopping while they are hot and thirsty and the hard pavements hurt their feet. They are uncomfortable, but four other people are unhappy: Jenny because her parents have been killed in an accident, Amy and Bob because they have no child of their own, and Kevin because he is leaving school with no job to go to. But into their lives comes a mysterious clown and through him they are all helped to have a happy Christmas.

Margaret Beames loves getting letters from children who have read her books. She also enjoys visiting schools as part of the Writers in Schools scheme and is quite willing to travel far away from her home in Feilding. When she is at home she sits down at her desk every day between 10 am and 2 pm, writing books, plays and articles. First of all she writes in longhand, then she corrects and improves until she finally types on the word processor she was recently awarded. She says it is not important whether she has any ideas when she goes to her desk. Her advice to anyone who wants to write is, 'Sit down and write *something*. It may be good, it may not. But it's the only way to get started. If you just sit there thinking you'd like to be a writer, you won't be!'

BIBLIOGRAPHY

Books for children

Fiction

The Greenstone Summer. Reed, Wellington, 1977.
Hidden Valley. Mallinson Rendel, Wellington, 1983.
The Plant that Grew and Grew. Illus. Donna Hoyle. Ashton Scholastic, Auckland, 1984.
The Parkhurst Boys. Mallinson Rendel, Wellington, 1986.
Clown Magic. Mallinson Rendel, Wellington, 1989.
The Little Spider. Shortland, Auckland, 1990.

Snow Goes to Town. Shortland, Auckland, 1990.
Three Plump Pigeons. Nelson Price Milburn, Wellington, 1990.
Juno Loves Barney. Thomas Nelson, Melbourne, 1990.

Books for adults

Karen: Her Fight against Leukaemia (with Karen Scotson).
   Dunmore Press, Palmerston North, 1988.

JUDY CORBALIS

Born Dannevirke. She has one grown-up son and lives in London.

Pets Three Burmese cats. She once bred Burmese and had seventeen kittens in the house all at one time! She also has two poodles: Titus, a standard size, and Bigsby, a miniature. When they are not being wicked they are loving and cuddly!

Favourite food Rather a lot of things, but especially ice-cream. Judy lives close to one of the best ice-cream shops in the world. Sashimi (Japanese raw fish) is also a favourite.

Favourite pastimes Reading, working on inventions, listening to modern classical and electronic music, cycling, travelling, swimming and dogs.

Favourite authors As a child: P. L. Travers's *Mary Poppins*, Richmal Crompton's William books and stories that her grandparents read to her including *The Iliad* and *The Odyssey*.

Likes Sunny weather, visiting schools with friendly children, big roaring fires in winter, and her friends.

Dislikes Parsnips and beetroot, people who are cruel to animals or people, going to the dentist, and Titus and Bigsby running into ponds then shaking themselves all over her.

Profession A teacher of English, then an actress.

Judy Corbalis became a writer quite literally by accident. The accident occurred after she had left teaching in New Zealand and gone with her family to London. There she decided to take a course at the London Academy of Music and Dramatic Art. She had always wanted to act and she had taken singing lessons, so she did well and was given roles with the Handel Opera Group.

She was really on the road to success when, on the way to a rehearsal, she stopped to buy some lunch — a pizza and an orange juice. She drank the juice and suddenly it seemed as though her throat was on fire. Some cleaning fluid had been left in the orange juice container and it burned her throat so badly that for six months she could not speak at all. It took much longer to get her voice back to normal.

It was a cruel accident. Just as she was doing so well she had to stop. What use is an actress who cannot speak or sing? She could not even return to teaching. How could she teach with no voice? She remembers it as one of the most depressing times of her life. But Judy Corbalis is not one to sit and do nothing for long. Perhaps if she could not talk she could write. But what? As a teacher she knew how important it is to read stories to children of all ages. She herself had grown up with stories. Not only had her grandparents read aloud to her, but her father had told her a story every night of her life until she was at high school. She says, 'I feel deeply sorry for any child who misses out on being read to. I still remember it and I still love being read to. I think most people do.'

So she decided to write the sort of stories she would like to read aloud to children. But they would also have to be ones she herself would enjoy. 'That's what's so much fun about being a writer,' she says, 'you're always writing yourself stories.' Because she had always been fond of fairy tales she thought she would try to write a fairy story with a modern twist.

The result was *The Wrestling Princess and Other Stories*. The wrestling princess is six feet tall, wrestles with the palace guards and drives a forklift truck. The seeds for the story had been sown when Judy was a child and had wanted to drive a steam roller. Her mother told her that she would never be able to because girls 'didn't drive great big machines'. This excuse annoyed Judy and so in her very amusing stories girls and women lead adventurous lives.

In 'Georgiana and the Dragon' (in *The Wrestling Princess*) it is the princess who rescues the prince from the clutches of the dragon rather than the other way around. In 'The Enchanted Toad', another story in the same book, the Queen has run away to be a racing driver. In Judy Corbalis's first novel, *Oskar and the Ice Pick*, Oskar's mother is a mountaineer while his grandmother, who had been a ballerina in her youth, is now a champion underwater swimmer.

The original for Oskar's grandmother was one of Judy's grandmothers. She had been very modern for her time. She wore a bikini before anyone else did, went out to work when most women worked at home, and loved dressing up and wearing glamorous clothes. Judy says, 'She never worried about anything we did. She simply assumed we were naturally sensible and wouldn't come to any harm if she didn't supervise us.' She even wanted to be called by her first name, like Elspeth, the grandmother in *Oskar and the Ice Pick*.

At the beginning of the book Elspeth receives a singing telegram:

I have an invitation
For a swimming race,
And in just two days
It will be taking place.
The Queen has asked especially
If you'll please compete
In the new Grandmothers' Cross-Atlantic
Underwater Feat.

This is an invitation she cannot refuse, but it means that she will be unable to take Oskar's mother's ice pick to the Himalayas, where she is mountaineering. So Oskar and Henrietta, the singing telegram girl, take the ice pick instead.

Now you may have noticed that on Judy Corbalis's list of favourite foods she rates ice-cream very highly. She would find it as much of a disaster as Henrietta and Oskar do, when they arrive in the Himalayas to discover a dastardly plot to commandeer all the ice-cream in the world. To save ice-cream for children everywhere they have to foil a fiendish scientist and a wicked governess, not to mention overcome difficulties with yetis.

A less eccentric grandmother appears in the picture book *The Cuckoo Bird*, illustrated by David Armitage. This grandmother was modelled on Judy's kindly, comfortable, story-reading grandmother. She warns her granddaughter to let no one into the house while she is away, but when the girl discovers a baby on the doorstep she carries it inside, little knowing that it is really the wicked cuckoo bird in disguise. Needless to say, when the grandmother returns the problem is sorted out.

Judy Corbalis's love of lively language is especially evident in her picture book for older children, *Porcellus the Flying Pig*. Porcellus is able to fly because he was born with strange bumps on his back. Judy Corbalis says, 'I have always had very big sticking-out shoulder blades that I was acutely conscious of when young. My grandfather used to tell me they had wings in them. I'm sure one day it will be possible to fly just by stretching out and lifting off and I hope it's in my lifetime.'

Having decided to write a book about someone able to fly she thought it would be fun to have a flying pig. Fun too, to make puns on words connected with pigs, of which there seem to be a surprising number. Take the names of PORCellus's brothers and sisters: SOWphie, HAMphry, HOGden, STYmon, PIGby, SPAMela and AlBOARtine, amongst others.

The young Porcellus turns out to be very musical and is

taught the cello by his godmother, Cider-Bess Bacon. But secretly he worries that the bumps on his back make him different from the others. He decides to earn enough money to have them removed by a surgeon. So he is interviewed by the manager of Porclay's Piggy Bank, none other than J. Rotting-Pigswill himself, and is given a job as night-watchman. But one night the bank is broken into by the terrible gangster Al PORCone. The book is made even more memorable by Helen Craig's hilarious illustrations.

Judy Corbalis is not at all interested in writing what she calls 'improving' books. She says she wants her books for children to be fun, but if there is a message in *Porcellus* it is to not be afraid to be different. She worries that sometimes children can be put down for what is called 'showing off', when they should be able to enjoy their talents and abilities.

She is certainly enjoying her own. At present, as well as inventing stories, she is inventing things. This is because her next book is about two inventors, Mr and Mrs Fooby-Lartil, and she is actually constructing some of the things they invent. These include the Fooby-Lartil Rain-Proofed-Banana-Peeler, the All-Purpose-Multi-Child-Invent-Your-Own-Music-Machine and the Fooby-Lartil Long-Term-Domino-Knock-On-Knock-Down-Mouse-Terrifier, and some inventions too secret to reveal!

She writes longhand in exercise books, then types on the word processor. She loves lots of different pens with different colours and varying nib thicknesses and uses them all. She rewrites a huge amount. After she had rewritten *Oskar and the Ice Pick* thirteen times the editor came and took the manuscript away and wouldn't let her have it back!

Judy Corbalis believes that you should have a go at whatever you want to do. She says, 'If you think you might be a good artist or stock-car racer or dancer you should try it and if you find out you aren't so good, it doesn't matter. It's nice to enjoy life.' It's good advice and, coming after all the ups and downs of Judy Corbalis's career, it's worth listening to.

BIBLIOGRAPHY

The Wrestling Princess. André Deutsch, London, 1986.

Oskar and the Ice Pick. André Deutsch, London, 1988.

Porcellus the Flying Pig. Illus. Helen Craig. Cape, London, 1988.

The Cuckoo Bird. Illus. David Armitage. André Deutsch, London, 1988.

Your Dad's a Monkey. André Deutsch, London, 1990.

JOY COWLEY

Born   Levin, 7 August 1936. She has four children and lives near Picton.

Pets   A black and white furry purry friend cat called Took, who is nineteen years old. A golden dog named Honey, who is lazy and affectionate. A bossy goose, Beatrice, and fifty-five sheep!

Favourite food   Everything! But especially ice-cream.

Favourite pastimes   Reading, fishing, boating, white-water rafting, spinning, knitting, cooking, eating.

Favourite authors   As a child she read adventure stories — James Fenimore Cooper, R. M. Ballantyne, Victor Hugo, Alexandre Dumas, Rafael Sabatini, Jules Verne. Present-day favourites are Margaret Mahy and Russell Hoban. 'Both these writers extend me beyond myself into new countries of the mind.'

Dislikes   'Cuddly language in children's books — the author talking down to children.' She believes authors should write for children as they write for other adults, but within children's experiences. She would like to see children have more say in library selections and children's book awards.

Profession   Writer.

Awards   NZ Children's Book of the Year 1983 for *The Silent One.*

If you were lucky enough to learn to read with cheerful, well-told story books, the chances are that Joy Cowley wrote some of them. One look at the list of her books will show just how many she has written and how many publishers she has worked for. But does writing beginner-reader stories mean that the author is a 'beginner writer'? Certainly not. Joy Cowley has written a prize-winning novel for older children as well as longer picture books, and she is very well known as an adult novelist.

Why, then, does she now spend so much time writing easy-to-read books? It is because she passionately believes that reading is *very* important indeed. If you cannot read you cannot enter into the wonderful world of books. That world not only leads to knowledge about every subject but it can also open up wider vistas of the imagination — what Joy Cowley calls 'new countries of the mind'. Because she believes that reading is the key that opens the door to so many possibilities she wants to help children to read. She does this by supplying stories written in language that is fun and will encourage children to enjoy reading.

Her first children's book, *The Duck in the Gun*, was published as long ago as 1969 in the United States. It was hardly known in New Zealand until a new edition with Robyn Belton's wonderful and amusing pictures came out in 1984, but it quickly became one of the most famous and best loved of New Zealand children's stories.

It tells how a General, about to besiege a town, finds that a duck has made a nest in his cannon. Although he is quite prepared to blow up the town and everyone in it, he does not like to disturb the duck, and so the war has to be put off until the ducklings have hatched. But by this time the soldiers have made friends with the townspeople and the General is in love with the Mayor's daughter! It is a very amusing book but it has a serious side, because it shows how absurd it is for people who could really like one another to wage war.

Several of Joy Cowley's books are about resolving conflicts peacefully. In *Brith the Terrible* a stranger with a box of butterflies gets rid of a giant who has frightened the town for years. The giant, it seems, is very ticklish and butterflies are very good at tickling! *Captain Felonius* manages to stop swearing when he learns to write down the forbidden words instead of saying them, with some surprising results. In *The Fierce Little Woman and the Wicked Pirate* the fierce little woman refuses to be bullied by a wicked pirate who wants to enter her house. But then she discovers that even wicked pirates are afraid of the dark...

Those villains are not entirely bad and are reformed characters by the end of the story, but in *Salmagundi* there are two really wicked villains. They are a woman called Dr Foster and a man named Major Brassblow. She owns a factory that makes missiles to blow up tanks. He makes tanks to shoot down missiles. The smoke and smog from their factories make the towns miserable places but, of course, Dr Foster and Major Brassblow do not live there. They have splendid mansions well away from the city.

For a long time they tell the people that they are only making these weapons to keep the peace. But a strange series of events causes them to turn from manufacturing armaments into making licorice allsorts and hats. The smog lifts, the townsfolk are happy but this, unfortunately, is not the end. 'True wickedness does not lie quiet for long,' says Joy Cowley, and before long Dr Foster and Major Brassblow are up to their old tricks again.

Dr Foster and Major Brassblow are human monsters, but monsters of a different kind feature in *The Terrible Taniwha of Timberditch*. In this story Josephine wants to trap a taniwha. To do this she needs a spade to dig the trap, an apple to put in it, and some string. While shopping for these items she meets Scottish, Greek, Chinese and Norwegian shop keepers and learns about their monsters. The Scots have the Loch Ness monster, the Greeks have the gorgon, the Chinese have dragons, and the Norwegians have trolls. 'A monster is only what you think it is,' she says.

So far *The Silent One* is Joy Cowley's only novel for older children. She says it was the result of a number of different factors, which all 'came together'. She had been asked to write a story about deaf children and she very much wanted to do this because her own father, who had recently died, was profoundly deaf. It was while she was turning over the idea of a story for the deaf that she went on holiday to Fiji and there saw a beautiful old turtle in the Nadi marketplace. Suddenly everything fitted. She even had her typewriter with her and straight away she started the beautiful story of Jonasi, the silent one.

He is silent because he is deaf and has never been able to hear anyone talking. His coming to the island had been mysterious. As a baby he had been found by the captain of a boat, drifting in a little canoe in the middle of the ocean. Some of the village people said he would bring bad luck but old Luisa, who longed for another child, loved him and adopted him. Gradually it became clear that the child could not talk and that was another reason the villagers thought he was strange and blamed him for any misfortune. In his unhappiness Jonasi turns for comfort to a beautiful white turtle, which he discovers in an offshore pool. But when a hurricane devastates the island the people again blame Jonasi and try to kill the white turtle. The story is written with such deep feeling and compassion that no one who has read it will ever forget it.

The Silent One has been made into a film, and Joy Cowley tells amusing stories of the difficulties they encountered in making it. In one scene there is a pig hunt, but the film makers found it very hard to get a pig. Pigs are important property in Fiji and no one wanted to give theirs. Another problem was that the electric generators on the island were not big enough to power the fans that made the strong winds needed for the hurricane. In the end they had to use the down-draught from a helicopter, but no one watching the absorbing story unfold on screen would realise the problems that had to be overcome.

Joy Cowley loves the sea and now lives in the beautiful Marlborough Sounds, near Picton, where she can enjoy fishing and boating. She even sees her stories as fish: 'Ideas are the bait which catch stories. Don't ask me where the stories come from. They are the mysterious fish which swim in the sea of imagination.'

Some of her ideas may have been stored up from her childhood, when she used to read all the time. She would even cycle to school with a book propped up on the handlebars. Once she ran into the back of a stationary van and did considerable damage to both herself and her bike. If she was not reading stories, she was telling them to her sister at night, long after the lights were out. She says they were serials that went on week after week, like soap operas. Even then, it seems, she was enthusiastic about reading and story telling — a pastime that has brought so much pleasure to her and to her many readers.

BIBLIOGRAPHY

Books for children

The Duck in the Gun. Illus. Edward Sorel. Doubleday, New York, 1969. New edition (illus. Robyn Belton), Shortland, Auckland, 1984.

The Silent One. Whitcoulls, Christchurch, 1981.

The Terrible Taniwha of Timberditch. Illus. Rodney McRae. OUP, Auckland, 1982.

Two of a Kind (with Mona Williams). Blackberry Press, Upper Hutt, 1984.

The Fierce Little Woman and the Wicked Pirate. Illus. Joe Davies. Shortland, Auckland, 1984.

Salmagundi. Illus. Philip Webb. OUP, Auckland, 1985.

Brith the Terrible. Illus. Deirdre Gardner. Shortland, Auckland, 1986.

Captain Felonius. Illus. Elizabeth Fuller. Shortland, Auckland, 1986.

The Lucky Feather. Illus. Philip Webb. Shortland, Auckland, 1986.

My Tiger. Illus. Jan van der Voo. Shortland, Auckland, 1986.

Books for adults

Nest in a Falling Tree. Secker & Warburg, London, 1967.

Man of Straw. Secker & Warburg, London, 1971.

Of Men and Angels. Hodder & Stoughton, London, 1973.

The Mandrake Root. Hodder & Stoughton, London, 1976.

The Growing Season. Hodder & Stoughton, London, 1979.

Heart Attack and Other Stories. Hodder & Stoughton, Auckland, 1985.

Women Writers of New Zealand 1932–1982 (editor, with Thelma France). Colonial, Wellington, 1982.

Readers

29 Story Chest Books for Shortland, Auckland, 1981–82.

24 Story Chest Ready-Set-Go Books for Shortland, Auckland, 1981–82.

24 Story Chest Read Together Books for Shortland, Auckland, 1982–83.

5 Story Box Books for Shortland, Auckland, 1982–85.

13 Story Chest Ready to Read Books for Department of Education School Publications Branch, Wellington, 1982–87.

16 Story Chest Get Ready Books for Arnold Wheaton, Leeds, 1983.

30 Jellybeans Books for Shortland, Auckland 1985–88.

63 Sunshine Books for Heinemann, Auckland, 1986–87.

8 Windmill Books for Heinemann, Auckland, 1986–88.

Old Tuatara. Department of Education School Publications Branch, Wellington, 1983.

The King's Pudding. Shortland, Auckland, 1986.

Turnips for Dinner. Shortland, Auckland, 1986.

Mrs Grundy's Shoes. Shortland, Auckland, 1986.

70 Kilometres from Ice Cream. Department of Education School Publications Branch, Wellington, 1987.

Giant on the Bus. Shortland, Auckland, 1987.

RUTH DALLAS

Born Invercargill, 29 September 1919, as Ruth Mumford. Dallas is a pen name. She had two sisters, five and ten years older than she was, and now lives in Dunedin.

Pets As a child, the family owned a big brown dog, a tortoiseshell cat that got stuck up ladders and a duck that ate all her pet tadpoles.

Favourite food Speckled bananas and juicy apricots.

Favourite pastimes Reading, gardening and listening to serious music.

Favourite authors As a child she liked Gene Stratton Porter's *Girl of the Limberlost*, *Grimm's Fairy Tales*, *Tales of King Arthur*, Bunyan's *Pilgrim's Progress*, Emily Brontë's *Wuthering Heights*, Mark Twain's *Huckleberry Finn*, L. M. Montgomery's Anne books and Charles Dickens.

Dislikes Noisy neighbours who disturb her when she is listening to music!

Profession Writer.

Awards NZ Literary Fund Achievement Award 1963. University of Otago Robert Burns Fellowship 1968. NZ Book Award for Poetry 1977. Buckland Award for Poetry 1977. Litt D (University of Otago) 1978.

Ruth Dallas says that she has been writing for as long as she can remember. By the time she was nine she had copied out all her stories and poems onto blue writing-paper and fastened the pages into a book with red cord taken from a Christmas card. By the time she was twelve she was sending work to the *Southland Daily News* (later the *Southland Times*), which published two whole pages of children's writing every Saturday. She sent stories or poems to the paper every week until she was eighteen and was too old to be considered a child.

At that time the editor of the *Southland Times* was Monte Holcroft (father of Anthony Holcroft, another author in this book). He started publishing her poems and later on she was also published in the New Zealand *Listener* and in the literary magazine *Landfall*, where for five years she worked as secretary to the editor, Charles Brasch.

Because her poetry was so successful she was awarded the Robert Burns Fellowship, which gives a writer enough money to live and work at the University of Otago for a year. At last she had time to do something she had wanted to do for years, and that was to write novels for children. She had already written stories and poems for the *School Journal*, but she particularly wanted to write longer books set in New Zealand, because when she was growing up in Invercargill all the books she read had come from England or North America. She had learned about big cities, upstairs bedrooms, villages and very old houses, but neither she nor her friends had ever read stories about early New Zealand.

She wanted to write about people like her own great-grandparents, who had come to New Zealand in 1851 and had lived in a pioneer cottage on the banks of the Avon, before the city of Christchurch was built. Her own grandmother Dallas, whose name she took for her pen name, had lived with them when Ruth was young and had told many stories of the things that had happened when she was a nurse in the last century. She was the model for the mother in Ruth Dallas's four books, *The Children in the Bush, The Wild Boy in the Bush, The Big Flood in the Bush* and *Holiday Time in the Bush.*

All of them are about a family who lived in Southland in the nineteenth century, near the sawmill where their father had worked. He died when the youngest, Jean, was only a baby and the mother, who is a nurse, has to go out to work to keep the family by looking after sick people in the village or on nearby farms. Because their mother is often away from home, the four children have various mishaps, although in general they are very good and responsible. Jean, the youngest, is the story teller and she describes incidents such as how their cow, Hokey-Pokey, strays into a swamp, and how they discover a man who has been seriously injured by a falling tree.

One of the children's favourite walks is on the tram track, along which newly cut timber for the sawmill is towed by a sturdy little engine, the Puffing Billy. Their walks often lead to interesting discoveries. One time they happen across a beautiful limestone cave, on another occasion they find moa bones. An even more exciting discovery is that of a 'wild boy' named Barney, who has neither home nor parents and lives in a cave.

Later books in the series feature a flood, a chimney fire on Christmas Day, and a very eventful pet show. The picture given in these books is very vivid because the characters are so real and, although they have few modern comforts, there is always a great deal of fun and laughter. Ruth Dallas was surprised by how successful the novels became overseas. They were not only published in Great Britain and the USA but also translated into Swedish, Danish and German. She says she suddenly discovered that the stories were 'not only about New Zealand children, after all, but about children everywhere'.

Ruth Dallas always writes warmly about dogs and in another book, *A Dog Called Wig*, this time set in the present day, she has written what must be one of the world's most unusual animal stories. But the beginning seems very familiar. A boy,

Archie, wants a dog. Imagine his dismay when he is actually allowed to keep a stray dog, but the dog attaches itself to his father instead of him! There is a happy ending, but not before Archie is involved with some escaped borstal boys and the dog has been injured.

Perhaps having a grandmother living in the house when she was young has made Ruth Dallas particularly sympathetic to older people. Several of her poems and two of her novels feature the elderly. The old lady in her poem 'Grandmother and Child' could well be the old lady in her book *The House on the Cliffs*. In the poem:

The waves that danced about the rock have gone,
The tide has stolen the rock as Time has stolen
The quiet old lady who waited beneath the trees
That moved with a sad sea sound in the summer wind.

In the book old Biddy Bristow is often misunderstood because she lives alone and seems different. 'She wore a long brown overcoat and fisherman's hat and walked along the beaches carrying a bag and a rake.' When the children ask her what she is looking for she replies, 'A bell to ring when the wind blows.'

Two girls, Brenda and Judith, think that Biddy is a witch, but when Brenda delivers some groceries to her she finds that the old woman is simply lonely. She has no one to talk to except her pets, a young albatross and a sheep called Patch. Because she is old and unusual the local people want to put her in an old people's home. But Biddy could not bear to be shut away. 'I'm like the albatross and I have to be free,' she says in the book.

How Brenda and Judith help her to stay in her own home and how they discover the secret of the bell make this a very memorable story, which is perhaps the closest of Ruth Dallas's novels to her poetry. The beach where Biddy searches for the bell is like the one in the poem 'Deserted Beach':

If there had been one bird, if there had been
One gull to circle through the wild salt wind
Or cry above the breaking of the waves
But. . . only the sea moved there
And weeds within the waves like floating hair.

In *Shining Rivers* Ruth Dallas brings together her interest
in the early settlers and her sympathy for old people. The book
is set in Otago in the 1860s, where Johnie Crawford, aged
fourteen, has just arrived in Dunedin with his mother. His
father died on the journey out from Edinburgh so his mother
has to get a job and works as a maid. Johnie goes to work
at a bakery but there he catches 'gold fever' and nothing will
satisfy him but to go to the diggings. He wants to earn enough
money to buy a piece of land for his mother and himself.

But life in the gold fields is tough. Johnie is robbed several
times and would not have survived without the friendship of
an old gold prospector, Tatey. Tatey is a splendidly independent
old man and he and Johnie stay together for years, so that at
last Johnie learns that some things are more valuable than gold,
and that friendship is one of them.

BIBLIOGRAPHY

Books for children

Fiction
The Children in the Bush. Methuen, London, 1969.
Ragamuffin Scarecrow. Otago University Bibliography Room,
    Dunedin, 1969.
A Dog Called Wig. Methuen, London, 1970.
The Wild Boy in the Bush. Methuen, London, 1971.
The Big Flood in the Bush. Methuen, London, 1972.
The House on the Cliffs. Methuen, London, 1975.

Shining Rivers. Methuen, London, 1979.
Holiday Time in the Bush. Methuen, London, 1983.

Non-fiction
Sawmilling Yesterday. Department of Education, Wellington, 1958.

Poetry for adults

Country Road and Other Poems. Caxton Press, Christchurch, 1953.
The Turning Wheel. Caxton Press, Christchurch, 1961.
Experiment in Form. Otago University Bibliography Room, Dunedin, 1964.
Day Book: Poems of a Year. Caxton Press, Christchurch, 1966.
Shadow Show. Caxton Press, Christchurch, 1968.
Song for a Guitar and Other Songs (edited by Charles Brasch). University of Otago Press, Dunedin, 1976.
Walking on the Snow. Caxton Press, Christchurch, 1976.
Steps of the Sun. Caxton Press, Christchurch, 1979.
Collected Poems. University of Otago Press, Dunedin, 1987.

JOAN de HAMEL

Born   London, 31 March 1924. She has five sons, and lives on the Otago Peninsula.

Pets   Numerous over the years — at present donkeys and goats.

Favourite food   Preparing too many meals over the years has left her not at all interested in food!

Favourite pastimes   Tramping, bird-watching, reading.

Favourite authors   Children's: Jane Gardam, Philippa Pearce, Jill Paton Walsh, Penelope Lively. Adults': Patrick White, Chaim Potok.

Profession   Teacher. From 1967 to 1979 she was a lecturer in French at Dunedin Teachers' College.

Awards   NZ Library Association Esther Glen Award 1979 for *Take the Long Path*.
A. W. Reed Memorial Award 1985 for *Hemi's Pet*.

If ever you are waiting at an airport or travelling on a boat you may notice someone busily writing in a notebook. You risk glancing over her shoulder, she catches you looking at her and starts writing in French instead. The chances are that you are watching Joan de Hamel in action.

She began the habit of taking notes on people, places and events when she was a child travelling all over Europe with her parents and her sister in a tiny Austin car. Visiting different countries also sparked her interest in foreign languages and when she was fifteen she was sent to a French-speaking school in Switzerland. She says, 'Since I was incapable of remaining silent, I became fluent very swiftly.' She went on to study French at Oxford University and then to teach it, although she always wanted to write and continued to keep her notebooks.

But marriage to her doctor husband, Francis, and the arrival of three sons kept her far too busy to write in England. Even after they emigrated to New Zealand in 1955 there was little time for writing, because two more sons were born here. She continued to keep her notebooks, however, and at last the day came when the youngest boy went to school and she could concentrate on shaping all the information she had accumulated.

A novelist has to *feel* a story as well as note the characters and where it takes place, so it is not surprising that Joan de Hamel's first book was about a time when she had been very frightened. She and her husband became lost in the South Island's remote Kepler Mountains while they were bird-watching. They could not be certain that they would find their way out of the bush or that anyone would find them, and they needed all their knowledge of bush craft to survive. So do the family of two boys and a girl in X Marks the Spot. They are going on holiday to Fiordland, when the helicopter taking them from Te Anau crashes, injuring the pilot. They have to start walking out of the dense bush to get help. Fortunately they are well equipped — until they lose their backpacks crossing a river.

X Marks the Spot is an exciting story, made vivid by Joan de Hamel's real knowledge of the bush. She lovingly portrays the high peaks and the dancing sunlight and shadow of the foliage, but she also shows the dangers. There are rivers that flood, the misery of being bitten by thousands of hungry sandflies and the real worry of being so far away from the safety and comfort of home.

The children in X Marks the Spot accidentally stumble upon

a plot to smuggle the rare kakapo out of the country, and all three of Joan de Hamel's novels feature New Zealand's endangered species. In her second book, *Take the Long Path*, it is the yellow-eyed penguin that plays an important part in the story. This book was also sparked off by a traumatic experience. She had been watching the rare penguins coming back from the sea to their nests in the sandhills of the Otago Peninsula when she saw one that had been savaged by a shark. She watched with horror as it died and she noted how shocked its mate was and how it grieved.

She used this incident in *Take the Long Path*, when the central character, David, has to help the unhappy mother penguin to rear her chicks after her mate is killed. In doing so he begins to understand some of his own family problems. He is further helped by a mysterious old Maori man who sets him the task of discovering an ancient patu, or whalebone club. The three strands of the plot — the family difficulties, the search for the club and the penguins — are all cleverly woven together by the end of the story, which won the Esther Glen Award in 1979.

Joan de Hamel enjoyed researching Maori history for the book. She thinks that it is perhaps because she is an immigrant that she is so anxious to find out all she can about New Zealand, its plants, its trees, its animals and its past. 'I must know the past of anywhere I live,' she says. 'When I study the past I understand the present. I always *liked* New Zealand, but now that I have learned more about it I *love* it.'

Because she loves New Zealand so much, especially the Otago Peninsula where she lives, Joan de Hamel worries that its rare and very special animals may disappear. In her latest novel, *The Third Eye*, she turns her attention to the tuatara. The three children whom we first met in *X Marks the Spot* are four years older and now, as teenagers, they set about stopping the illegal smuggling of tuatara into the USA. They are being taken by an American scientist who wants to test her theory that the reason the tuatara can survive on barren rocks is its third eye. She feels this might give the key to survival after nuclear war. Like Joan de Hamel's other books, there is more to this novel than just the story. The setting is Golden Bay, in the north of the South Island, where people want to 'develop' the area for property and industry. Is it wrong to develop an area if it will result in more jobs? But what if the development means destroying the native bush and its birds and animals?

These are the problems the young people in Joan de Hamel's novels have to consider. They are, of course, the sort of problems that have to be confronted in life. Being the mother of five sons means that she is well aware of the difficulties that young people face but, she says, 'Life is an adventure. There are obstacles to overcome and then we move on to the next challenge.' She finds her own challenges in writing. The detailed descriptions in her notebooks do not easily turn themselves into novels with lively and believable characters. She writes in longhand, revising again and again to 'turn the muddle into shape'. She says, 'If it's true that the test of a vocation is the love of the drudgery it involves, then I must qualify as a writer with a vocation.'

Pets have always been an important part of Joan de Hamel's life. But *Hemi's Pet*, her only picture book, is about a very unusual pet — none other than Hemi's little sister. He insists that she is a pet because he lives with her and looks after her. But the de Hamels have plenty of animal pets because they breed donkeys and goats. Every morning Joan sweeps out the sheds and this simple action seems to clear her mind. She plans her books as she works and talks about them to the animals. She says they are good listeners and never offer unwanted advice!

BIBLIOGRAPHY

X Marks the Spot. Lutterworth Press, Guildford, 1973

Take the Long Path. Lutterworth Press, Guildford, 1978.

Hemi's Pet. Illus. Christine Ross. Reed Methuen, Auckland, 1985.

The Third Eye. Viking Kestrel, Auckland, 1987.

ANNE de ROO

Born   Gore, 23 September 1931. She lives in Palmerston North.

Pets   There have always been pets in her life, at least a cat and a dog. She has a budgie in her study.

Favourite food   She likes all food — especially if someone else cooks it. She particularly likes cake and ice-cream and fancy puddings with lots of whipped cream — but not too often!

Favourite pastimes   Gardening, when she can find the time and can find the garden among the weeds. She enjoys learning new things.

Favourite authors   So many it is difficult to decide. As a child she loved George McDonald's *At the Back of the North Wind*.

Likes   Beautiful things, whether mountains or pottery, animals or people.

Dislikes   Intolerance.

Profession   She has always done work that would give her some money but also time to write. Past jobs include being a library assistant, a governess (in England) and a secretary.

Awards   ICI Bursary 1981.
Choysa Bursary for Children's Writers 1982.
NZ Children's Book of the Year 1984 for *Jacky Nobody*.

When Anne de Roo was nine years old her family moved from the South Island to New Plymouth. Close to the new house was a wild river, which she loved. With her little black dog she spent as much time as possible there, swimming, exploring and making up stories. One of the stories she told herself was that one day she would become a famous writer of dog stories. This has come true because, although not all her books are about dogs, animals do play a very important part in them. They often give comfort to someone who is lonely or who feels in some way an odd-one-out.

Her very first novel, *The Gold Dog*, starts with a boy, Jonathan, who is teased because he is different and loves reading. At school he is called 'Bookworm' and 'Rosebud'. He has few friends and longs to have his own dog, but he has no money to buy one. Still, he lives in Otago near the old gold diggings and in his reading he learns about panning for gold. He follows the instructions, discovers two nuggets of gold, and buys his dog. He also earns great respect from his classmates.

Another odd-one-out is Boy in *Boy and the Sea Beast*, because he is the only male in his family of mother, two grandmothers and seven sisters. But when a taniwha comes into the harbour Boy, as the man of the family, has to swim out to ask it to go away. As it turns out the creature is not a taniwha but a dolphin, whom Boy names Thunder. Thunder becomes a great favourite, just as the famous dolphin Opo had been, but Boy starts to worry that Thunder may share the same fate as Opo and be harmed by all the publicity. In a story that is both funny and sad, Boy takes matters into his own hands.

Tessa Duggan, in *Cinnamon and Nutmeg*, is a Taranaki farmer's daughter. She loves working on the dairy farm and her father proudly calls her his 'farm boy'. But when a baby brother arrives on the scene Tessa realises that her father has always wanted a son, not a daughter. Deeply hurt, she finds comfort in a new puppy and then in rearing a calf and a goat. The same characters appear in the sequel, *Mick's Country*

Cousins. Mick is sent to work on the farm instead of going to borstal, after he is involved in stealing a car. He feels odd because he looks like his Maori father but has been brought up by his Pakeha mother. He feels European, yet everyone treats him as though he is Maori. Gradually, through caring for the animals and getting to know some of the farm people, he begins to understand that your race matters less than who you are.

The Taranaki bush is the setting for *Scrub Fire*, in which three children get lost and have to survive in remote countryside after they have run away to escape a bush fire. Not long after she had completed the book a friend suggested to Anne de Roo that she should write something about James Mackenzie, the sheep stealer. She was referring to the famous story of the Scotsman who, with his remarkable collie dog, drove a herd of stolen sheep and discovered what is now called the Mackenzie Pass. Mackenzie was put in prison but was finally pardoned and left for Australia. No one knows for certain what happened to the dog.

Needless to say, with her interest in dogs, Anne de Roo did her level best to find out the truth. She read as much as she could but found nothing about where the dog had gone while Mackenzie was in prison. For her own satisfaction she decided to write a book about what might have happened, and the result is *Traveller*. As she says, 'In the end, Mackenzie hardly came into the story at all — it is all about the dog.' The story is set in the 1850s and one of the reasons *Traveller* is Anne de Roo's own favourite is that she so much enjoyed doing the research. She decided to find out more about the past and her next novel, *Because of Rosie*, is again about early settlers.

Anne says that all her books begin with her wondering, 'What would happen if . . .' and before she wrote *Because of Rosie* she started wondering what would happen if a family of orphans set out to walk from Wellington to the Manawatu. What sort of people would they be, living through the hardships of 1872? The story grew out of the characters, who are ordinary people, not famous like Mackenzie or Hone Heke, the Maori leader who features in *Jacky Nobody*.

Knowing Anne de Roo's interest in the odd-one-out, it is not surprising that once she became attracted to the story of Hone Heke she decided to see it through the eyes of an unusual boy, Jacky Nobody. Jacky believes that he is the son of Pakeha missionaries who had died. But when he meets the warrior Hone Heke he is greeted as tama (son or nephew). Puzzled by this, he asks his adoptive parents who he really is and learns the truth — that his father was a sailor who left his Maori wife and son soon after Jacky's birth. The realisation that he is part Maori comes as a shock to Jacky. He feels that he is neither Pakeha nor Maori, that he is a 'nobody'. In the war that follows Hone Heke's cutting down of the flagstaff at Kororareka, Jacky does not know what to do. Should he stay with his adoptive parents and his cheeky Pakeha friend Noah? Or should he join his kinsman Hone Heke?

The book has a sequel, *The Bat's Nest*, which is set in the days before Hone Heke's final defeat. Anne de Roo admits that the most difficult writing she has ever done was about the battles. She read four or five different accounts of each one and found it extremely hard to visualise where everybody was and what they were doing. 'I hated doing those,' she says. But she had enjoyed the other research, reading through diaries, books and newspaper articles of the period.

Her latest book, *Friend Troll, Friend Taniwha*, moves a long way from battle scenes in the war-torn Bay of Islands. When talking about it, she explains how sometimes a book can take a very long time from getting the first idea to being written down. The idea for *Friend Troll, Friend Taniwha* came when she was driving across a little bridge on the way to Napier. The friend who was with her said, 'Isn't this just the sort of bridge a troll would be sitting under waiting for billy goats?' Anne de Roo realised that they were between Dannevirke and Norsewood, exactly where the Scandinavians had settled. If

51

there was a troll in New Zealand, it would be under that bridge.

At the time she wondered briefly what would happen if a Norwegian troll met a Maori taniwha, but it was not until five years later, when she was in the middle of redecorating her cottage, that thoughts of trolls and taniwha drifted into her head. What if a baby troll had climbed into the luggage of a Norwegian immigrant? He would most certainly have grown too big to keep in a house. Where would he go? The place for trolls must be under bridges. Would he be homesick? Would he remember Billy Goats Gruff, Norwegian fiords and pine forests? What would happen if a taniwha came along?

By the time she had finished redecorating, the delightful and very amusing story was already in place in her mind and she enjoyed writing it down. Because for Anne de Roo writing has always been a way of talking to other people. She explains, 'A writer is always saying, "Hey, look what I've just found out. Isn't it exciting?" And the fun is that you never know who you're saying it to. It's great when you meet someone you've never met before and they say, "Your book talked to me."'

BIBLIOGRAPHY

The Gold Dog. Hart Davis, London, 1969.
Moa Valley. Hart Davis, London, 1969.
Boy and the Sea Beast. Hart Davis, London, 1971.
Cinnamon and Nutmeg. Macmillan, London, 1972.
Mick's Country Cousins. Macmillan, London, 1974.
Scrub Fire. Heinemann, London, 1977.
Traveller. Heinemann, London, 1979.
Because of Rosie. Heinemann, London, 1980.
Jacky Nobody. Methuen, Auckland, 1983.
The Bat's Nest. Hodder & Stoughton, Auckland, 1986.
Friend Troll, Friend Taniwha. Hodder & Stoughton, Auckland, 1986.

LYNLEY DODD

Born Rotorua, 5 July 1941. She has two children, and lives in Wellington.

Pets Many over the years. Currently a rat, an eight-year-old blackbird, and a cat, Pipi.

Favourite food Mushrooms.

Favourite pastimes Reading, listening to music, being outdoors and travelling.

Favourite authors As a child she enjoyed Dr Seuss and A. A. Milne, but now her favourite children's authors are Quentin Blake, Joan Aiken and Margaret Mahy. She loves biographies, Tolstoy, Jane Austen and Patrick Campbell.

Likes Auction sales, nonsense and wildlife programmes.

Dislikes Pomposity, lumpy porridge, earthquakes. She is not too fond of hairy spiders.

Profession She taught art before her family arrived. Now writes and illustrates full time.

Awards NZ Library Association Esther Glen Award 1975 for *My Cat Likes to Hide in Boxes.*
Choysa Bursary for Children's Writers 1978.
NZ Book Award for Illustration 1981 for *Druscilla.*
NZ Picture Book of the Year in 1984 for *Hairy Maclary from Donaldson's Dairy*, in 1986 for *Hairy Maclary Scattercat*, and in 1988 for *Hairy Maclary's Caterwaul Caper.*

One day when Lynley Dodd was looking in her ideas book, among the lists of words, newspaper cuttings and drawings she found a sketch she had made three years earlier of a shaggy dog. Underneath it she had written

One morning at 9, on his way to the park
Went Hairy Maclary from Donaldson's Dairy.

It suddenly struck her that this might be the germ of a picture book, and she started drawing and writing. The result was one of New Zealand's most famous stories, *Hairy Maclary from Donaldson's Dairy*.

Hairy Maclary himself was a mixture of several dogs she knew and she added friends for him, Bottomley Potts the dalmatian, sheepdog Muffin McLay, the greyhound-like Bitzer Maloney, not to mention the dachshund Schnitzel von Krumm with the very low tum and Hercules Morse as big as a horse. But as they all trot down to town they meet the formidable cat Scarface Claw...

Scarface Claw was modelled on the Dodds' own black cat Wooskit, although in reality Wooskit was a much kinder cat than the tough Scarface. He had also been the model for the cat in *My Cat Likes to Hide in Boxes*. This was her first book and her cousin, author Eve Sutton, wrote the text.

Until *My Cat* was so successful, Lynley Dodd had always thought of herself as an illustrator. She had, after all, trained as an artist and taught art in schools, but she began to think it would be fun to write her own book, as well as doing the pictures. In any case, she now had her own children who were always wanting her to tell them stories.

The first book she both wrote and illustrated was *The Nickle Nackle Tree*, about birds. Her house in Wellington is surrounded by native bush and she loves watching the birds that come to it. As a joke she had one day done a cartoon for an architect friend, of numerous birds all standing on one another's heads. She had called it 'High Rise Birds in an Urban

Environment', but she realised it could be turned into a picture book. It began:

In the Manglemunching Forest there's a Nickle Nackle tree,
Growing Nickle Nackle berries that are red as red can be.
I went to look last Monday; I was too surprised for words
— On every twisty branch there was a jumbly jam of birds.

The birds include a Ballyhoo bird, Scritchet birds, Tittle Tattle birds, and Snooze and Huffpuff birds, as well as the Chizzle and Natter varieties.

The amusing language and pictures show that Lynley Dodd was influenced by one of her own childhood favourites, Dr Seuss. They also show that she is not only a gifted artist but also a clever writer. This is a very unusual combination of talents. Most people are either good at writing or good at art. Very few (Beatrix Potter was one) can produce their own picture book in which the story and the pictures work together to make a very satisfying whole.

Her next book, *Titimus Trim*, was about an old gentleman who got his housework mixed up. It came about, she says, because she was trying to look after two children as well as write books. This was particularly difficult because she was working on the dining-room table and it had to be cleared for every meal. She is very happy now because she has a large desk in a sunroom extension of the living-room. It is usually covered in books, papers, pens, brushes, the telephone, a lamp and a stuffed toy Hairy Maclary, not to mention a cat, so there is scarcely room to work, but at least she does not have to remove it all every time the family wants to eat.

Almost all Lynley Dodd's books are about animals. She respects them enough to keep them in character as animals and does not turn them into 'honorary humans'. Birds perch in branches, dogs steal bones and cats get stuck up trees. It is not surprising to find that television wildlife programmes are among her favourites.

The Smallest Turtle came about because the family had seen a rather sad 'Our World' programme that showed turtles having to get to the sea from their hatching place in the burning sun. One turtle became confused and went inland by mistake. This upset her children, so to try to cheer them up she said, 'I shall write a turtle story with a happy ending.' And she did.

The possum who stole the apple in *The Apple Tree* was, sadly, all too true. It was their tree, their apple and a very real possum who stole it. Even *Wake Up Bear*, in which all the animals try to waken the bear from hibernation, is not so far from reality. After all, a bee's buzzing might well excite a bear with thoughts of honey.

But of all her books, the Hairy Maclary stories have proved the most popular, and because there need be no limit on Hairy Maclary's friends and acquaintances we can hope for many more yet. *Hairy Maclary's Bone* was inspired by seeing a large labrador carrying off a bone from the butcher's shop. *Rumpus at the Vet* came about because she was taking her cat to the vet's and saw a large cockatoo in a cage. She started wondering, 'What if . . .' and the result was a whole new collection of animals, including Custard the Labrador, Noodle the Poodle and the delightful Poppadum kittens from Parkinson Place. They are sure to appear in a later book, just as Slinky Malinki (also based upon Wooskit), whom we first met in *Scattercat*, now has a book to himself.

It is a sad fact that many things that look easy, such as a perfect dive, or a beautiful shot in tennis, only come about after hours of practice. The same is true of writing and painting. Lynley Dodd says that she writes endless drafts of her stories 'in longhand on mountains of paper'. She sometimes returns to draft nine after reaching draft fifteen. Her pictures, too, have been drawn and redrawn to make it look as though she had simply sat down and drawn them straight away.

There are so many details to consider. For *Hairy Maclary's Bone*, she says, 'I had to buy a bone and plan carefully to get the right size and shape to fit Hairy's mouth. I drew the bone in all sorts of positions and from every possible angle. Then I made it into soup!'

She continues, 'I work on words and pictures together from the start. As I write I'm thinking about and planning the layout of the book. Once that is done I make a small "dummy" to show what the finished book will be like with everything in place. Then I paint the final pictures full-size.'

Lynley Dodd is thrilled that children all over the world think of Hairy Maclary as 'their dog'. In letters she receives she finds that English children think he lives there, Americans write about him 'on sidewalks' and Australians put him among kangaroos. It is this universal appeal that places these books among world favourites for their delightful language and lively pictures. But, she says, 'We New Zealanders all know that those letterboxes in Hairy Maclary are definitely Kiwi ones.'

BIBLIOGRAPHY

The Nickle Nackle Tree. Hamish Hamilton, London, 1976.

Titimus Trim. Hodder & Stoughton, Auckland, 1979.

The Apple Tree. Mallinson Rendel, Wellington, 1982.

The Smallest Turtle. Mallinson Rendel, Wellington, 1982.

Hairy Maclary from Donaldson's Dairy. Mallinson Rendel, Wellington, 1983.

Hairy Maclary's Bone. Mallinson Rendel, Wellington, 1984.

Hairy Maclary Scattercat. Mallinson Rendel, Wellington, 1985.

Wake Up Bear. Mallinson Rendel, Wellington, 1986.

Hairy Maclary's Caterwaul Caper. Mallinson Rendel, Wellington, 1987.

A Dragon in a Wagon. Mallinson Rendel, Wellington, 1988.

Hairy Maclary's Rumpus at the Vet. Mallinson Rendel, Wellington, 1989.

Slinky Malinki. Mallinson Rendel, Wellington, 1990.

Lynley Dodd has also illustrated the following:

My Cat Likes to Hide in Boxes (by Eve Sutton). Hamish Hamilton, London, 1973.

Pussyfooting (by Jillian Squire). Millwood Press, Wellington, 1978.

I'm a Tree (by James K. Baxter). Price Milburn, Wellington, 1979.

Druscilla (by Clarice England). Hodder & Stoughton, Auckland, 1980.

Kindness and *Barnyard Song* (traditional). 1981.

Pop, Pop, Pop (by Beverley Randell). Methuen Educational, Auckland, 1981.

One Big Dinosaur (by Beverley Randell). Methuen Educational, Auckland, 1981.

The Pesky Paua (by Robin Cunningham and Fran Hunia). Price Milburn, Wellington, 1983.

TESSA DUDER

Born   Auckland,
   13 November 1940. She
   has four daughters, and
   lives in Auckland.
Pets   At present she has
   one dog and one cat, but
   in the past pets have
   included ducks, hens,
   hamsters, guinea pigs and
   even a seagull.
Favourite food   Summer
   fruit, particularly melons.
Favourite pastimes   Music, sailing, reading, swimming.
Favourite authors   She admires Margaret Mahy,
   Philippa Pearce, Penelope Lively, Leon Garfield,
   Katherine Paterson, Ivan Southall and Jan Mark.
Dislikes   The Americanisation of New Zealand
   culture, and the way everything is measured in
   terms of dollars.
Profession   Before she married she was a journalist.
Awards   Choysa Bursary for Children's Writers 1985.
   NZ Children's Book of the Year 1988 for *Alex*.
   NZ Library Association Esther Glen Award 1988
   for *Alex*.
   NZ Children's Book of the Year 1990 for *Alex in
   Winter*.

As you walk into Tessa Duder's sitting-room you immediately
notice a large grand piano laden with music, then your gaze
turns to the view through large windows to sailing boats on

Auckland's Lake Pupuke. It comes as no surprise to find that her interests are music, sailing, reading and swimming, and that those are just the subjects she writes about.

Tessa Duder was brought up in Auckland, where her father was a doctor but also a fine pianist who had debated whether to study music or medicine. Her mother had been a professional cellist before giving up a musical career to get married. It was a happy house, full of music, and Tessa, like the heroine in *Alex*, was a lively, outgoing girl who enormously enjoyed her time at Diocesan School. She was enthusiastic about English and history, acted and sang in school productions, and represented the school in swimming. She started specialising in the butterfly stroke, which few other swimmers were tackling, and while still at school she became the New Zealand champion, going on eventually to represent New Zealand at the Empire (now Commonwealth) Games in Cardiff, Wales, in 1958.

There the similarity to Alex ends. Tessa had no major rival like Maggie. She did not have disagreements with officials, and she did not break a leg or lose a boyfriend. But she does remember sleepless nights before a big race and the punishing hours of training. *Alex*, then, is not an autobiography. Tessa Duder has simply done what all good writers do, which is to draw on their own experiences but then to ask, 'What if this...or that...had happened?'

The Alex books grew out of her knowledge of competitive swimming, and an earlier novel, *Jellybean*, reflects her interest in music. Her sister-in-law is a professional violinist and for a while Tessa played the piano with her in a trio that gave concerts and performed at private functions. It made her realise how difficult it must be to be a mother who has all the worries of getting dinner or having a sick child at home, yet still has to look calm and elegant and play well *every night*. She wondered how it would feel to be the child of such a mother and Geraldine — or Jellybean — was the result. *Jellybean* was

Tessa Duder's second book. Her first book, called *Night Race to Kawau*, drew on her interest in sailing.

She is married to John Duder, a great-grandson of the first European settler in Devonport, who is a keen amateur sailor. But there was no opportunity to go sailing when they were first married because they lived in Pakistan, where John worked as a civil engineer on a dam on the Indus River. Their first three daughters were born there, and a fourth arrived after their return to New Zealand when John was working in Tokoroa. It was not until they returned to Auckland that they were able to go sailing again. They now own a splendid old kauri gaff-rigged cutter, the *Undine*, which was the first Fullers Cream Trip vessel used in the Bay of Islands, and which had always been a working boat.

Because Tessa Duder did not herself come from a sailing family she had to learn about boat handling from the beginning. She began to see how important it is to work as a team, and as a result she has been very active in the Spirit of Adventure Trust, sometimes acting as a volunteer mate on the beautiful tall ship *Spirit of Adventure*. The Trust enables school children to go to sea for ten days, a time that is often as important for its effect on character as its teaching of seamanship.

Before her marriage Tessa Duder had worked as a reporter in Auckland and in London but she had never thought of writing children's books. The idea was given to her one day when she wanted to send a New Zealand children's book to friends in Pakistan. It was the late 1970s and there were very few. When she complained about this the bookshop assistant said, 'Why don't you write one?' It so happened that her youngest daughter had just started school and for the first time in years she had some spare time.

But what should she write? She turned to her own experience. Her husband knew a great deal more about sailing than she did, and she had often wondered how she would manage if anything happened to him when they were at sea. So she wrote *Night Race to Kawau*, in which the mother and children have to manage when the father is injured. It is made doubly exciting because the race takes place at night, when darkness complicates matters. One result of working on the book was that she decided to do a Boat Masters course and has become a very competent sailor.

Tessa Duder's knowledge of boating and of the Waitemata Harbour, combined with her interest in the past, have led her to write a number of non-fiction books, which are of equal interest to adults and children.

The great success of her Alex books has meant that she is much in demand as a speaker, as a judge of awards, and as a member of the Children's Book Foundation. Yet she still finds time to sing in a choir, to accompany the choir at a local school, to play the piano and to read.

It is difficult to find enough hours in the day, but she has organised herself as much as possible. An answerphone protects her from callers in working hours and she finds a word processor has revolutionised her writing. It means that she has to plan the structure of the book, rather than letting it happen as it goes along, but once the chapters are outlined she finds she can do four drafts on the screen and only needs to make one final copy. This allows her to work much faster, which is good news for her enthusiastic readers, who look forward to many more books.

BIBLIOGRAPHY

Fiction
Night Race to Kawau. OUP, Auckland, 1982.
Jellybean. OUP, Auckland, 1985
Alex. OUP, Auckland, 1987.
Alex in Winter. OUP, Auckland, 1989.

Non-fiction

Discovering Kawau. Bush Press, Auckland, 1981.

The Book of Auckland. OUP, Auckland, 1985.

Spirit of Adventure: The Story of New Zealand's Sail Training Ship. Century Hutchinson, Auckland, 1985.

Waitemata: Auckland's Harbour of Sails. Century Hutchinson, Auckland, 1989.

3 readers for Shortland, Auckland, 1986–88.

BEVERLEY DUNLOP

Born   Nelson Province, 25 August 1935. She lives in Napier.

Pets   She loves animals and once bred Persian cats. She now has one cat, black with a white whisker, named Rum Tum, and a chihuahua called Pedro.

Favourite food   Whitebait and crayfish.

Favourite pastimes   Playing and listening to music, reading, growing orchids and lilies, and travelling.

Favourite authors   As a child: Charles Kingsley's *Water Babies*, Kenneth Grahame's *The Wind in the Willows*. As a teenager: Emily Brontë's *Wuthering Heights*, poetry, and the novels of Charles Dickens and Jane Austen. As an adult: Russian writers such as Leo Tolstoy and Mikhail Sholokhov, and New Zealand authors Maurice Shadbolt and Janet Frame. Children's writers she now enjoys are Richard Adams, Ruth Park and Roald Dahl.

Dislikes   Loud screaming music, quarrels, cruelty to children and animals. She feels strongly about destruction of forests and wildlife, and hates driftnet fishing and whaling. She can't bear to kill anything, not even garden and household pests.

Profession   Writer.

Awards   Choysa Bursary for Children's Writers 1982.

As Beverley Dunlop grew up music and writing were her great passions. She longed to play the piano and finally started learning at the age of twelve. She played classical music for hours and decided to become a music teacher. She took Trinity College examinations and while studying for her Letters she took a few pupils. She then discovered that she hated teaching music so much that she did not even bother to sit her final exams. She became a legal secretary and because she is such a good typist she can compose her stories directly on the typewriter.

Beverley Dunlop calls herself a 'short-term expert'. This is because as soon as she gets an idea for a book she feels she must discover everything there is to know about the subject. She didn't, for instance, know a great deal about dolphins until she went to live in Napier, but there she met Frank Robson, who had written *Thinking Dolphins, Talking Whales*. He believes that dolphins are not only intelligent but also wise. Beverley Dunlop felt she would like to write a story about dolphins, but they presented a problem. She didn't really want 'talking' dolphins and yet she wanted them to be able to communicate. The answer seemed to be to invent someone who could understand them. So in her book *The Dolphin Boy* there is a boy who knows the language of dolphins and is able to explain their extraordinary powers of communication and of healing to two boys who have become his friends. The three of them then discover a plot by some fishermen to kill the dolphins for taking their fish . . .

The Dolphin Boy is set in Anawai, which is really Napier, and Napier is also the setting for another of Beverley's novels, *Earthquake Town*. On 3 February 1931, Napier had been largely destroyed in one of the worst New Zealand earthquakes and there are still people living who remember the event very vividly. Once Beverley Dunlop had decided she would like to write about the earthquake, she found out all she could about it and interviewed people who could remember it.

She spoke to one man who had been at school when suddenly the building rocked and fell down about him. A number of his school friends were killed and he had great difficulty in getting back to his own home. Beverley Dunlop thought how terrible it would be to have your school destroyed, your friends killed and not even to know whether your parents were alive. *Earthquake Town* is based on people's experiences in Napier, here called Clifton. The central character, Megan, is daydreaming in class, making up a story about herself as 'Mighty Megan', when the earthquake strikes. The book describes how she leaves her ruined school and tries to find her parents on that terrible day.

A very different kind of research was needed for her latest novel, *Spirits of the Lake*. She had visited Lake Waikaremoana in the Urewera and the whole area stirred up many childhood recollections. She remembered how her father, a dairy farmer in Takaka, had turned up some ancient Maori greenstone tools when he was ploughing a field. Some of them had dark markings and she had wondered whether the marks were blood spilled in battles long ago. She had always been fascinated by stones. As she wandered along the beaches of Golden Bay she would collect beautiful, patterned pebbles, and sometimes she would rub them to see whether she could call up spirits, the same spirits who supposedly haunted the caves of Takaka and the mysterious old tree on the river bank.

Now in the Urewera that sense of the presence of spirits was reawakened and she started to read all that she could about the area and particularly about the Maori leader Te Kooti. She wondered whether she could write a story about him and about the legend of Lake Waikaremoana, which tells how a chief's daughter was punished for disobedience by being turned into stone. But could she make old stories seem exciting to present-day readers? Perhaps events should be seen through the eyes of one of them? So she describes how the hero, Paul, finds a mysterious stained stone hidden in his grandparents' old clock.

The discovery of the stone leads to a series of dramatic and unpleasant events: a car accident, strange behaviour from his mother and sister and his own extraordinary dreams.

One book Beverley Dunlop did not have to research was *The Poetry Girl*, which is based on her own childhood, growing up in Nelson Province and then moving to the Waikato. Like her, the heroine, Natalia Olga Kondrotovitch, grows up near Nelson and moves to the Waikato. Her age is the same as Beverley Dunlop's, twelve in 1947 and fifteen when the book ends in 1949. The story recounts her unhappiness at school and how she found comfort in reading, and particularly in reading and memorising poetry.

Like Natalia, Beverley started writing her own stories at an early age. But the first time she tried to get one published she suffered a setback. 'I thought it was the best story in the world,' she says. 'I put it in an envelope and sent it away to a magazine. For weeks afterwards I went out to the letterbox every day to see if the magazine editor had accepted the story. One day I did get a letter — the editor had sent the story back!'

After the first disappointment she realised that the editor was right, that the story was not as good as she had thought and that perhaps she should *learn* how to be a writer. She started writing articles about interesting people. She learned to be a good listener. Much of what she wrote was returned to her but she kept writing and at last one day the editor of the *New Zealand Woman's Weekly* accepted an article.

Beverley Dunlop then joined a group of writers who invited visiting speakers to talk to them. One speaker was the editor of the *School Journal.* He suggested that they should try to write some stories for the *School Journal* and, although she had never written for children, she decided to try. In 1975 she sent the editor her first story, 'Little One', and since then she has written more than eighty stories for the *School Journal.*

Many of them are about the animals she knew and loved as she was growing up on the farm. One story, 'The Turkey

Dog', is about a dog called Don, who loves turkeys and is very gentle with them, although he is quite fierce with cows. That story and others about a cat, a horse, a mouse, a pukeko and a pig have now been collected into *Queen Cat and Other Stories*. All of them first appeared in the *School Journal.*

Beverley Dunlop is not sure whether she will continue to write for children. She would quite like to write for adults again. She is anxious not to get 'stuck' with writing for any one age group or on any one subject. She would get bored if she had to produce 'formula' books, she says.

One very wide subject, however, will never cease to attract her, and that is New Zealand itself. Its countryside, its animals, its seaside, its history and its myths have an endless fascination. She wonders whether her Russian father's passionate love for his 'Mother Russia' has given her a particular love for her own native country and a longing to write about it. There is certainly plenty in New Zealand to keep her busy, researching to become a 'short-term expert' for every book she decides to write.

BIBLIOGRAPHY

Books for children

The Dolphin Boy. Hodder & Stoughton, Auckland, 1982.
The Poetry Girl. Hodder & Stoughton, Auckland, 1983.
Earthquake Town. Hodder & Stoughton, Auckland, 1984.
Spirits of the Lake. Hodder & Stoughton, Auckland, 1988.
Queen Cat and Other Stories. Hodder & Stoughton, Auckland, 1988.

Books for adults

Profile of a Province: Hawke's Bay (with Kay Mooney). Hodder & Stoughton, Auckland, 1986.

BARRY FAVILLE

Born Hamilton, 16 April 1939. He has three children, two boys and a daughter. He lives in Taupo.

Pets Cats.

Favourite food Oysters.

Favourite pastimes Gardening (especially growing things to eat), fishing, tramping,

and listening to classical music, especially Vivaldi. He likes 'mild' jazz, but nothing later than the 1960s. He works in strict silence.

Favourite authors Children's: Robert O'Brien, Peter Dickinson and Rosemary Sutcliff. Adults': William Faulkner's books and history and science books written for the layperson.

Profession Teacher. ·

Awards NZ Children's Book of the Year 1987 for *The Keeper*.

Barry Faville jokes that he took up writing novels to avoid jogging. When he was teaching in Singapore from 1981 to 1983 he watched with horror as the craze for jogging grew, even in the sticky heat of an equatorial climate. He had to make up a good excuse for not doing it!

Joking apart, sooner or later Barry Faville would almost certainly have turned to writing. His house is full of books and he studied English at Auckland University. Much of his working life has been spent teaching English. He is interested in ideas and in the many ways in which they can be expressed. He is, above all, a communicator, whether in teaching, writing or broadcasting.

One of his first jobs, after a brief spell of teaching at Glendowie College, Auckland, was in broadcasting for schools and as a script writer of Radio New Zealand's spoken features. Later, after he had returned to teaching, he wrote a series of non-fiction articles for the *School Journal* called 'Fighters for Freedom'. He wanted to feature people who had become famous without having to resort to violence or war, people like Socrates and Gandhi.

The results of violence and war feature in two of his three novels. The first, *The Keeper*, is set at some time in the future, when the central North Island has been devastated by both a nuclear war and a volcanic eruption. The second, *The Return*, sees visitors from outer space coming to Earth to discover why its inhabitants spend so much money and energy on manufacturing dreadful weapons of destruction.

The idea for *The Keeper* first came to Barry after he read Jonathan Schell's *Fate of the Earth*. This set him wondering what would happen in Taupo, where he lives and teaches, after a disaster. The story is told by a young man, Michael, who is learning to be a scribe. His teacher, Mr Clinton, is anxious that the knowledge accumulated by our civilisation should not be lost. With no printing presses, everything has to be written down. Rather like a mediaeval monk, Michael has to copy everything by hand.

The world has gone back to a primitive existence. Groups of people live in isolation, and they are suspicious not only of one another but also of anyone who dares to be different. The Big Lake (Taupo) people do not altogether trust the Mud Pool (Rotorua) folk. All of them distrust the Loners, wandering people who are the descendants of those who had been genetically damaged by radiation.

Barry Faville enjoyed writing *The Keeper*. His experience on radio enabled him to create different voices for the characters. Each one has an individual way of speaking and writing. Michael's style is not as polished as Mr Clinton's. This meant experimenting with different ways of writing, something Barry Faville is able to do because he is a very fine craftsman.

The idea that writing is actually a craft, not just inspiration, comes to Robbie, the central character in *Stanley's Aquarium*, when she discovers an old poetry book with pencilled margin notes. Suddenly she realises that the poet Samuel Taylor Coleridge

> had sat down and cold-bloodedly put those words just where he wanted them. They had let him push them around. There had been no flash of inspiration from a friendly Muse. He had made the decisions and he had pushed and prodded until the stanza had clicked into place.

Barry Faville enjoys 'pushing and prodding' words into place. Writing every evening for ninety minutes in longhand, he shapes his work, aiming to produce 300–400 words in that time.

The starting point for his second novel, *The Return*, was another scientific book, *The Tangled Wing* by Melvin Konner. It is about the science of genetics, that is, how something in our bodies called DNA determines what we inherit from our ancestors — looks, intelligence, perhaps even temperament. Barry began to wonder what would happen if some superior race from outer space came to this world and conducted a genetic experiment on the inhabitants. Suppose there was 'a genetic transplant performed in the region of the brain that controls language'. Suppose 'the minds of human beings could be made to understand and use the techniques of thought transfer'.

This is exactly what happens in the novel, which is set at the end of the nineteenth century in a small East Coast community, Wilkes Beach. Fifty years later the visitors return to see the results of the experiment. They are particularly worried about

> the sudden appearance of firearms and weapons of all sizes, of a destructive power that far outstripped those we had last observed . . . The appearance of these new weapons was but one example of the advances that had been made. They also aroused fears about the state of mind of a race that could so eagerly invent and manufacture them.

They need to know whether this is the result of the experiment, or whether it is due to some other factor.

One of the most difficult aspects of writing fantasy or science fiction is to make extraordinary happenings seem believable. Barry Faville does this by causing the visitors to return in the form of a mother and son. The son attends the local primary school and makes friends with the headmaster's son, Jonathan Lockett. A vivid picture is given of life in Wilkes Beach, and particularly of the routines of the Lockett family at school and at home. But increasingly Jonathan feels that the new boy in his class seems to know exactly what he is thinking. . .

States of mind, the psychology of people, is obviously one of Barry Faville's great interests. Certainly the state of Stanley Swinton's mind is a key factor in his latest book, *Stanley's Aquarium*. The voice in this novel is that of the sixteen-year-old Robbie, and it clearly reveals that Barry Faville is well in touch with the students he teaches. The book describes what happens when she takes on a lawn-mowing job at the house of the strange Mr Swinton. He seems to be obsessed by South America and he has a mysterious aquarium, which she is not allowed to see. Apparently this aquarium is in some strange way going to threaten Lake Taupo. Mr Swinton tells Robbie, 'You are looking at one of the most dangerous places on the face of the earth.' It is Stanley Swinton who is dangerous, because he has never really outgrown his childish fantasies. By contrast, Robbie gradually grows from a rather uncertain adolescent to a balanced adult.

Lake Taupo has been the setting for two of Barry Faville's novels. As he lives and works near it and spends his leisure time tramping around it and fishing, his imagination is shaped by its beauty, but also by its dangers. Earthquakes could shake it, nearby mountains could explode as Mt Tarawera did. Everything could change. The landscape and the people offer a kaleidoscope of possibilities. We can only wait with interest to see where they will take Barry Faville in future.

BIBLIOGRAPHY

Fiction
The Keeper. OUP, Auckland, 1986.
The Return. OUP, Auckland, 1987.
Stanley's Aquarium. OUP, Auckland, 1989.

Non-fiction
Cook's First Voyage to New Zealand. Department of Education School Publications Branch, Wellington, 1969.

MAURICE GEE

Born   Whakatane, 22 August 1931. He has three children and lives in Wellington.

Pets   He has never owned a pet, although he loved his grandfather's dog. His favourite wild things have always been birds, and he hates seeing them in cages.

Favourite food   Almost anything, but he always has his own homemade porridge for breakfast, and is currently vegetarian. He recommends garbanzo and pumpkin casserole!

Favourite pastimes   Reading and walking.

Favourite authors   Charles Dickens and Saul Bellow.

Profession   Before becoming a full-time writer he was a teacher, then a librarian.

Awards   NZ Literary Fund Scholarship 1962, 1976.
Award of Achievement 1967, 1973.
University of Otago Robert Burns Fellowship 1974.
Hubert Church Prose Award 1973.
NZ Book Award 1976, 1979, 1982 and 1984.
James Tait Black Memorial Prize 1979.
Sir James Wattie Award 1979.
NZ Children's Book of the Year 1984 for
The Halfmen of O.
NZ Library Association Esther Glen Award 1986 for
Motherstone.
LitD (Victoria University of Wellington) 1987.

If you really want to annoy authors of children's books you ask them, 'Are you going to write for adults now that you are successful?' That is a dreadful question because it implies that adult books are more important than children's books, which they most certainly are not. In fact Maurice Gee was a highly successful author of adult novels before he started writing for children. When he became a full-time writer he wanted to broaden the scope of his books, and anyway his own children were always asking for stories.

But having decided that he would like to write a children's book, he began to wonder how on earth he should go about it. He had read very few stories for children. Although as a child Maurice loved reading, his father, a carpenter, had been unemployed for a long time and there was no money for books. There were few books in the school library and there was no public library in Henderson, Auckland, where they lived. In any case, when he was growing up there were really very few good writers for children. He remembers a book about Robin Hood but says, 'Nothing else took me completely into an imaginative world until I met Western stories at the age of thirteen. I lived in that world of six-guns and sage brush for several years until, in a kind of giant leap forward, I entered the world of Charles Dickens.'

It came as a wonderful surprise when, as an adult, he discovered Alan Garner's *The Weirdstone of Brisingamen*. He was fascinated by how the children in the novel were having to live in their everyday world and yet at the same time know that they were under terrible threat from another world, one that they could not share with adults.

He decided he would like to do something similar. But how? He explains: 'I wanted the story to take place in a world familiar to New Zealand children, so I chose Auckland and its volcanic cones. I had been reading a little about telepathic twins and decided to make use of that, and I made the twins redheaded because my daughters have red hair. But it was a long while before I found a story. Then one morning I was walking to work past Mt Eden. It was a drizzly day and the mountain was half hidden in a mist. As I walked up the street it seemed to crouch down and hide itself behind the houses. Then, at the end of the street, it suddenly loomed up and seemed to hang over me, and I found myself thinking, "I wonder what is living under there?" So, in that way, I found my story.'

The result was *Under the Mountain*, in which the redheaded Matheson twins have to combat strange creatures that are awakening from their long sleep beneath the volcanoes of Auckland, and which threaten to destroy the world. The book was later made into an exciting television serial.

An adult novel, *Plumb*, occupied his attention for a while, but when his daughter Emily was eight she wanted a story about a girl who wore glasses, as she did herself. At the time they were living in Nelson on a hillside overlooking the city. That view became the setting for *The World Around the Corner*, in which a girl finds some magic glasses belonging to another world, which is threatened by destruction.

Children from Earth are again involved in the trilogy *The Halfmen of O*, *The Priests of Ferris* and *Motherstone*. The idea for the first of these came when Maurice Gee was holidaying in Golden Bay, near Collingwood. He was walking up a little creek that flows into the Aorere River when he came across an old gold prospector using a homemade suction dredge. He says, 'I couldn't talk to him because of the hideous noise, and perhaps it was because of the noise that Jimmy Jaspers, who had his beginning in this old man, became such an unpleasant figure in the beginning. The following day, up the Kaituna, I came across a mine shaft sunk into the side of a hill. It was overgrown with ferns and had a rotted notice at the mouth warning people not to enter. This, I thought, made the ideal entrance to an imaginary world. The two things — the prospector, the shaft — came together, and the O books began.'

His own children again had some input into the stories. In

the first version of *The Halfmen of O* he was going to let Jimmy Jaspers fall off the cliff with Odo Cling and that was to have been the end of him. But his daughter said, 'No, no, you can't kill Jimmy!' So he rewrote the episode and saved him. He adds, 'It was a wise, not to say humane, decision. I don't think I would have had a trilogy without him.' Because, of course, Jimmy Jaspers, with Susan and Nicholas, becomes a central figure in the battle to save the world of O.

All Maurice Gee's fantasy novels move along at an exciting pace, but beneath the storyline there are strong messages that reflect his own views. Almost all his books are about the misuse of power. Among the things he most dislikes are 'Mad old men who think problems can be settled by dropping bombs...the military mentality is what I most dislike...I hate the way money, profit, has become the most important thing...I hate the greed that feeds on people. And the greed that feeds on natural things, which makes conservation...nuclear waste, poisonous chemicals and the felling of forests among my burning concerns.'

Anyone who has read the O books will quickly see that O, like our planet, is in danger from pollution, that the Priests in *The Priests of Ferris* have turned O into a police state and that in *Motherstone* there is the threat of nuclear weapons. Even in the earlier *The World Around the Corner*, Mrs Gates describes the evil Grimbles as having

> turned their half of the world into a desert. They have cut down the trees, levelled the hills, dammed up all the rivers. They live in great walled cities...their world is one of smoke and poison and darkness. They have factories making weapons. They fight among themselves.

It is only too easy to see that, unfortunately, in real life *we* are the Grimbles.

Both *The World Around the Corner* and the world of O have two halves that represent the forces of Good and Evil, constantly locked in deadly combat. The idea of parallel worlds perhaps reflects Maurice Gee's own interest in quantum physics, although his worlds are often very like New Zealand.

If one of the things he dislikes most is 'mad old men dropping bombs', his greatest love, apart from reading and writing, is walking in the hills with his family. He particularly likes rivers, and the family has invented a sport called river-walking. 'The dress for this is a bathing suit and an old pair of sneakers. We'd get in the middle of one of those lovely rivers in the hills at the back of Nelson and start walking up, swimming through deep pools, climbing up rapids and waterfalls, hand over hand . . . then down again still mid-river, to the starting point. Exhilarating, some of the best days I've ever had.'

It was his Auckland book *Under the Mountain*, however, that was first made into a television series. It was so successful that Television New Zealand asked him to write another serial. He decided to use material he had uncovered in 1978 when he was researching the history of Nelson Central School for their centennial celebrations. He had become fascinated by two interesting characters, 'a marvellous, enthusiastic, large-minded headmaster, who was interested in literally everything . . . and an arsonist who burned down many buildings around Nelson in the 1890s, including the school whose history I was writing.'

The result was the television serial 'The Fire-Raiser', which he set in the First World War. The fire-raiser himself is a farmer who upsets the children and their teacher by not allowing them to swim in a waterhole near his house. This is a mistake on his part because it leads to his unmasking. The small community is very well drawn and the terrible build-up of prejudice against a German woman is movingly portrayed.

The book *The Fire-Raiser* was actually written after the television script, and Maurice Gee thinks that he kept too closely to the script in the novel. When he came to write the book *The Champion*, after he had written the television serial, he decided to alter it slightly by having the principal character,

Rex, tell the story. This time the story is set in the Second World War in Kettle Creek — or Henderson, where Maurice Gee grew up. It is a time of shortages; petrol and sugar, for instance, are rationed, and Rex's father, the local barber, is not above selling things on the black market. The little community rubs along happily until three American soldiers arrive on leave, and one of them, Jackson Coop, is black. Like the innocent woman in *The Fire-Raiser* who is the victim of prejudice because she is German, Jackson Coop suffers because he is a Negro.

Both these novels are closer to Maurice Gee's adult books. They are what television producers call 'kidult' — an unflattering term that really means they will have universal appeal.

Only time will tell whether Maurice Gee's next novel will return to fantasy or science-fiction themes. He now lives in Wellington, closer to Parliament, and that should provide him with plenty of food for thought on the nature of power.

BIBLIOGRAPHY

Books for children

Under the Mountain. OUP, Wellington, 1979.
The World Around the Corner. OUP, Wellington, 1981.
The Halfmen of O. OUP, Auckland, 1983.
The Priests of Ferris. OUP, Auckland, 1984.
Motherstone. OUP, Auckland, 1985.
The Fire-Raiser. OUP, Auckland, 1986.
The Champion. Penguin, Auckland, 1989.

Books for adults

The Big Season. Hutchinson, London, 1962.
A Special Flower. Hutchinson, London, 1965.

In My Father's Den. Faber, London, 1972.

A Glorious Morning, Comrade. Auckland & Oxford University Presses, Auckland, 1975.

Games of Choice. Faber, London, 1976.

Plumb. Faber, London, 1978.

Meg. Faber, London, 1981.

Sole Survivor. Faber, London, 1983.

Collected Stories. Penguin, Auckland, 1986

Prowlers. Faber, London, 1987.

The Burning Boy. Viking, Auckland, 1990.

Non-fiction
Nelson Central School: A History. Nelson Central School Centennial Committee, 1978.

ANTHONY HOLCROFT

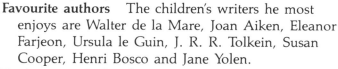

Born   Christchurch,
   14 November 1932. He
   has three children, and
   lives in Rangiora.
Pets   Always cats, because
   they are so cosy.
Favourite food   Cheese and
   Chinese.
Favourite pastimes   Reading,
   gardening, walking,
   listening to music and
   collecting early illustrated children's books.
Favourite authors   The children's writers he most
   enjoys are Walter de la Mare, Joan Aiken, Eleanor
   Farjeon, Ursula le Guin, J. R. R. Tolkein, Susan
   Cooper, Henri Bosco and Jane Yolen.
Profession   Orchardist.
Awards   Choysa Bursary for Children's Writers 1986.

It is sometimes hard to be the child of a famous father. Anthony
Holcroft's father, Monte Holcroft, was a very well-known
journalist, for many years editor of the *Southland Times* and
then of the New Zealand *Listener*. Anthony Holcroft grew up
in a home full of books and his father always encouraged him
to write. The young Anthony would fill journalists' notepads
with stories and leave them on the kitchen table for his father
to read. 'Not long ago I came across one of these notebooks
in a box of old manuscripts. It was filled with whimsical little
stories, jokes and drawings. I don't expect my father thought
they were very good, nevertheless his note in black pencil had

something kind and encouraging to say.'

But as he grew older he realised that he did not want to write the sort of stories his father expected him to write. His father encouraged him to read stirring tales about the past, such as G. A. Henty's. But a very different type of story interested Anthony. He wanted to read and reread fairy tales and myths. It seemed to him that they had stood the test of time because they were about unchanging things, such as the love of parent and child or of man and woman, and about how love can be killed by jealousy or possessiveness. Snow White's stepmother was jealous, Sleeping Beauty's father was over-protective.

Another thing that attracted Anthony Holcroft to traditional tales was that they were often mysterious. Something was always left for the imagination, even after the story had ended. Mystery had always appealed to him. As a child he was aware that some places seemed to have a special atmosphere — a magic — about them. A beloved grandmother had believed in spirits and he inherited from her a sense of the supernatural.

He became increasingly interested in stories about tree spirits or the strange Selkies. These are people who, in Scottish Highland mythology, live beneath the sea. When they are in the water they have seal skins. The Selkie women are very beautiful and when they come to shore to dance on smooth sandy beaches they lay aside their skins. Then, if any mortal man sees them, he must steal their skins. He could then force one of them to be his captive and to marry him.

The idea of loving someone and yet keeping them captive is a worrying one to Anthony Holcroft. He adapted the Selkie story to New Zealand circumstances in 'The Girl in the Cabbage Tree' (from *Tales of the Mist*). It tells how a lonely young farmer is out with his dog one day when it discovers a scarf,

> greyish in colour, lacy-looking, yet rough as well, like fine
> thread woven into a piece of bark fibre. It smelt salty, like

sea-weed and there was a damp spongy feel to it, as if the dew was on it. And when he held it up, it fell out in folds, like a skein, and he saw lights in it, blue and silver in the dusk.

Charlie takes the scarf home and before long its owner, a young woman named Nereda, comes to claim it. But Charlie refuses to let her have it, even though she marries him. He locks it up because he fears that once she has it back she will leave him. But the scarf is very important to Nereda and Charlie has to learn that loving someone means trusting them.

Anthony Holcroft says that the idea for this very memorable story first came to him one early morning when he watched mist floating like a scarf over the countryside. Perhaps that is why it is so vividly visualised and so deeply felt. He loves being out-of-doors, and that is where many of his ideas come to him. At one time he had thought about being a teacher and he studied English at Canterbury University, but he only taught for a short time because he decided that he preferred an open-air life. He started working on farms and now has his own orchard not far from Christchurch.

He loves working with trees because he feels that each tree has a presence and a life of its own. He particularly enjoys planting native trees, rather like Chen Li in his latest book, *Chen Li and the River Spirit*. Chen Li is granted a vision from the River Spirit of how the hillside had looked before the trees had all been cut down. 'I had shade, then, from the hot sun. My river flowed secretly under the trees, fish hid beneath its banks, and the forest was full of birds,' she says. She gives Chen Li some seeds to plant and he realises that he must devote the rest of his life to sowing a forest, although it means leaving his home and family.

It was perhaps the apple and pear trees in his own orchard that gave Anthony Holcroft the idea for an earlier book, *The Oldest Garden in China*, which features a beautiful pear tree.

The story develops because the Emperor cannot bear anyone's garden to be better than his. He is jealous and greedy.

These two faults often feature in Anthony Holcroft's stories. In 'The Night Bees' (from *Tales of the Mist*), Thomas and Janet Ryder live on a bush farm in the hills. But Thomas is greedy. Because he wants more money he works endlessly and neglects his wife. Finally he cuts down a grove of totara trees for profit and is punished by a swarm of bees, which nearly destroys his farm. Only then does he understand that 'true gold' is not in money but in the love that he and his wife have for each other.

The penalty for cutting down trees is a desert, and from these stories it may be seen that Anthony Holcroft is a keen conservationist. He knows the importance of trees.

Greed that destroys the environment is seen again in *The Old Man and the Cat*. The old man 'loved the forest and the creatures that lived in it but most of all he loved the birds'. He is overjoyed when all the birds of the island flock to hear his flute. It is a magic flute, made from strange driftwood. A cat also hears the music, sees how it attracts the birds, and steals the flute. At first it eats as many birds as it can, but then it discovers that there are no more birds — its greed has killed them all. *The Old Man and the Cat* is an example of what Anthony Holcroft calls 'the space needed for stories to grow'. He means that ideas often take a long time before they are finally ready to be written down.

The Old Man and the Cat had its beginnings when Anthony was fourteen, and it was his first attempt at writing a fantasy story. It was inspired by a cat that used to sit wide-eyed in front of their record player. Anthony Holcroft says, 'In the story I wrote, a black, skinny cat appears mysteriously at the home of an old man. Although it never seems to eat, it soon grows sleek and contented as it listens night after night to the old man playing his violin. But when the violin gets broken one day the cat begins to grow thin again and finally it drags itself away and is never seen again.' He continues, 'I put the story aside and forgot about it, but the idea must have gone on working underground because a long time later it surfaced again when I came to write *The Old Man and The Cat*.'

In *Rosie Moonshine* Anthony Holcroft returns to the theme of 'The Girl in the Cabbage Tree', that of trying to 'own' people. The idea for the story came to him one day when he was digging out a stone — just as the farmer Eric does in the book. 'At first the stone didn't seem to want to come out, but with a rocking and a tugging it finally came away with a soft hiss.' Anthony, like Eric, noticed 'a little puff of wind in his face and had a whiff of a sweet earthy smell, as if he had just unplugged a bottle of perfume'. It was almost as though a spirit had come out of the earth. In the book, Eric has released Rosie Moonshine, who works willingly for him but, like Charlie in 'The Girl in the Cabbage Tree', he fears losing her and he plugs the hole, with disastrous consequences.

You may have noticed that nearly all Anthony Holcroft's characters are farming folk, who work close to the land and close to their own families. Sometimes the life is hard. In 'The Island in the Lagoon' (from *Tales of the Mist*), poverty and illness cause Meg to leave her husband and farm to return to a fairy-tale floating island she had known in her youth. But her husband Michael searches for her and finds her. She returns home with him, although she knows that on the island 'she would have lived for ever beyond sickness and want, but if that had happened she would have been parted from Michael her husband, and that would have been a great sorrow'.

All Anthony Holcroft's stories are about caring — for people and for the environment. They linger in the memory partly because they speak to the heart, and partly because he has brought the Nameless Ones of mythology into the New Zealand landscape. Above all we remember them because he is a superb story teller who works his own special brand of magic upon us.

BIBLIOGRAPHY

The Old Man and the Cat. Illus. Fifi Colston. Whitcoulls, Christchurch, 1984.

The Oldest Garden in China. Illus. Fifi Colston. Whitcoulls, Christchurch, 1985.

Tales of the Mist. Reed Methuen, Auckland, 1987.

Rosie Moonshine. Illus. Lyn Kriegler. Century Hutchinson, Auckland, 1989.

Chen Li and the River Spirit. Illus. Lyn Kriegler. Hodder & Stoughton, Auckland, 1990.

ELSIE LOCKE

Born   Hamilton, 17 August 1912. She has four grown-up children, and lives in Christchurch.

Pets   She has no pets but enjoys bird watching.

Favourite food   Fruit — because it does not have to be cooked!

Favourite pastimes   Reading, swimming, tramping and bike riding.

Favourite authors   As a child she enjoyed Mark Twain's *Tom Sawyer* and Frances Hodgson Burnett's *The Secret Garden*. Of modern authors she enjoys Margaret Mahy, Rosemary Sutcliff, Jill Paton Walsh, Penelope Lively, Peter Dickinson and Tessa Duder.

Likes   Learning about anything new.

Dislikes   Caged birds. She is concerned about the lower standard of written and spoken English that she sees nowadays.

Profession   Historian and author.

Awards   Katherine Mansfield Award (*Landfall* magazine) for essay 1958.
Litt D (University of Canterbury) 1987.

Elsie Locke grew up in Waiuku, the youngest of a family of four. Although there was always enough to eat because they had home-grown vegetables and fish from the Manukau Harbour, the family was quite poor and there was little money left over. In those days secondary-school education was not compulsory. In fact, it was considered to be a luxury, especially for girls who would 'only get married'. There was certainly not enough money to buy books, so Elsie made up stories and told them to herself as she walked to and from school.

She was very excited when her father bought Arthur Mee's *Children's Encyclopaedia*, and they both read it from cover to cover. Elsie loved finding out about things and says that she still finds learning one of her greatest joys in life. Her teachers could see that she was a very clever pupil and when a high school was built nearby she was encouraged to go to it. She is grateful to the teachers there, especially the school's principal, Lincoln Garfield Smith. He realised that Elsie was starved for books and offered to lend her some. In the story of her early life, *Student at the Gates*, she tells how she first went to his house after she had been swimming.

I lingered before I opened the gate and knocked on the door. It was not the custom to be on visiting terms with teachers. But Mrs Smith was expecting me. She led me into the study, where I promptly slid into a chair and burst into tears! I had never imagined such riches! Apart from the window and the door, the room was entirely lined with books. Poetry, classics, modern novels, books on history and social change . . . were there in order and profusion. I don't remember what books I chose. I do remember more than once getting into trouble for being late home.

The 'riches' she discovered in this world of books decided her to go on to study at the University of Auckland. But those were the years of the Depression, and there were few grants available even to bright students. She had to earn money if she was to pay her way through university, so she worked as an assistant librarian, as a baby-sitter and by doing other people's housework.

It was while she was living and working in Auckland that

she saw for herself the results of unemployment and poverty. She became indignant that any government could allow such unfairness. She was determined to try to change things and so she became active in politics. She has been secretary of the Women Today Society, and from 1956 to 1965 she was a member of the National Committee of the New Zealand Campaign for Nuclear Disarmament. Today she is honoured throughout New Zealand for her work in the fields of peace and justice.

Her books reflect her interests. By the time she came to write her first novel she had married and was living in Christchurch, as she still does. You cannot live long in Christchurch without being aware of the early settlers. Every time you pass through Cathedral Square you see their names set into the paving stones. Many of the Canterbury settlers had come from wealthy English backgrounds, and brought money and possessions with them. But when Elsie Locke came to write a 'settler' story it was about a poor family. She says this was not because she deliberately set out to portray rather different settlers, but because she was excited by a true story that she heard about a Mrs Small. This woman had taken her children and run away from her drunken husband in Australia and had settled in Governors Bay, on the coast near Christchurch. It was the beginning of what was to become Elsie Locke's most famous novel, *The Runaway Settlers*.

When they came to New Zealand the Small family changed their name to Phipps and Elsie Locke vividly describes their struggles to get jobs, plant a vegetable garden and turn a dreadful rat-infested cottage into a comfortable home. Mrs Phipps is one of the strongest women characters in New Zealand children's books — she overcomes all difficulties and even drives a herd of cattle across the Southern Alps to the gold fields in Hokitika. All her children have their own adventures, but it is Mrs Phipps who stands out as the real heroine of the book. If ever you go to Governors Bay try to visit the peaceful churchyard, where you can see her grave.

Elsie Locke's training in history means that she loves to go to museums and libraries to look at old documents and to try to discover the real truth about the past. She had become very interested in the Land Wars because many of the disputes between Maori and settlers had begun around the Manukau Harbour, where she grew up. She wanted to find out the Maori point of view and in her next novel, *The End of the Harbour*, the main characters are an immigrant boy, David, and his Maori friend, Hone. Because David's parents keep a hotel in Waiuku they see all the comings and goings between the Maori and Pakeha leaders, but the book ends sadly.

A later book, *Journey Under Warning*, came about as the result of Elsie Locke's researching her own family history. She discovered that one of her own ancestors, William Morrison, had been involved in a land dispute over the Wairau Plain in the north of the South Island, which resulted in the local Maori asking Te Rauparaha to help them. The action is seen through the eyes of a fifteen-year-old boy, Gibby Banks, who accompanies William Morrison on a surveying party, and this book is perhaps more suited to readers of his age.

The most dramatic of Elsie Locke's novels is undoubtedly her account of one of New Zealand's most spectacular happenings, the eruption of Mt Tarawera in 1886. In *A Canoe in the Mist*, the canoe is the waka wairua, or ghost canoe, that appeared on the lake shortly before the eruption and which the Maori warned meant that some disaster was imminent.

Mt Tarawera actually blew up on the night when many astronomers were watching the conjunction of the moon with the planet Mars, and there were a number of visitors in Te Wairoa to see the event. The story is told from the point of view of two eleven-year-old girls, Mattie, visiting from England, and Lillian, whose parents keep one of the hotels. At first they are excited by what seems to be a marvellous display of fireworks, but later on they discover the dreadful consequences of the eruption. The mud rains down upon them, the Pink and White Terraces are destroyed, and worst of all, Te Wairoa itself is buried and many lives are lost.

In *Explorer Zach*, a book for younger readers, eight-year-old Zach explores a Canterbury farm in the 1920s and meets a number of interesting people. Elsie Locke has also written eleven non-fiction bulletins about the past for the Department of Education, as well as stories for the *School Journal*.

But her interests are not confined to the past. Books for younger children like *Look under the Leaves* and *Moko's Hideout* show her concern for New Zealand's unique wildlife, such as the paua, geckos, godwits and kea. Her love of tramping and of the outdoors is expressed in the adventure story she wrote with Ken Dawson, *The Boy with the Snowgrass Hair*, which outlines a number of expeditions in remote parts of the South Island mountains and bush.

Elsie Locke is one of the older writers featured in this book, but her interests and concerns are extraordinarily modern. She was one of the first writers for children to express opinions about the place of women in society, about injustices towards the Maori, about conservation and about the need to settle disputes peacefully rather than by conflict. She deserves a very special place in New Zealand's children's literature for her scholarship, her energy and her idealism.

BIBLIOGRAPHY

Books for children

Fiction
The Runaway Settlers. Blackwood and Janet Paul, Auckland, 1965.
The End of the Harbour. Blackwood and Janet Paul, Auckland, 1968.

Moko's Hideout. Whitcoulls, Christchurch, 1976.

The Boy with the Snowgrass Hair (with Ken Dawson). Whitcoulls, Christchurch, 1976.

Explorer Zach. Illus. David Waddington. Pumpkin Press, Christchurch, 1978.

Journey Under Warning. OUP, Auckland, 1983.

A Canoe in the Mist. Cape, London, 1984.

Non-fiction

A Land without a Master. Department of Education, Wellington, 1962.

Viet-nam. Department of Education, Wellington, 1963.

Six Colonies in One Country. Department of Education, Wellington, 1964.

Provincial Jigsaw Puzzle. Department of Education, Wellington, 1965.

The Long Uphill Climb: New Zealand 1876–1891. Department of Education, Wellington, 1966.

High Ground for a New Nation. Department of Education, Wellington, 1967.

The Hopeful Peace and the Hopeful War. Department of Education, Wellington, 1968.

Growing Points and Prickles: Life in New Zealand 1920–1960. Whitcombe & Tombs, Christchurch, 1971.

It's the Same Old Earth. Department of Education, Wellington, 1973.

Maori King and British Queen. Hulton, Buckinghamshire, 1974.

Look under the Leaves. Pumpkin Press, Christchurch, 1975.

Snow to Low Levels: Interaction in a Disaster. Whitcoulls, Christchurch, 1976.

Crayfishermen and the Sea: Interaction of Man and Environment. Whitcoulls, Christchurch, 1976.

A Land without Taxes: New Zealand 1800–1840. Department of Education, Wellington, 1979. Revised as *The Kauri and* the Willow. Government Printer, Wellington, 1984.

Two Peoples, One Land: A History of Aotearoa/New Zealand. Government Printer, Wellington, 1988.

Books for adults

Gordon Watson, New Zealander, 1912–1945: His Life and Writings (editor). NZ Communist Party, Christchurch, 1949.

The Shepherd and the Scullery Maid. NZ Communist Party, Christchurch, 1950.

The Human Conveyor Belt. Caxton Press, Christchurch, 1968.

The Roots of the Clover: The Story of the Collett Sisters and their Families. Privately printed, 1971.

Discovering the Morrisons (and the Smiths and the Wallaces): A Pioneer Family History. Privately printed, 1976.

The Gaoler. Dunmore Press, Palmerston North, 1978.

Student at the Gates (autobiography). Whitcoulls, Christchurch, 1981.

Poetry

The Time of the Child: A Sequence of Poems. Privately printed, 1954.

CAROLINE MACDONALD

Born   Taranaki, 1 October 1948. She lives in Australia.

Pets   She loves both cats and dogs. Matilda, and the basset hound and the scotch terrier, in *The Lake at the End of the World*, and Mex in *Visitors* are the only characters that existed in real life.

Favourite food   Almost anything Italian.

Favourite pastimes   Listening to music, singing in choirs, sometimes singing solo. She particularly likes music written in the seventeenth century. Reading is another favourite pastime.

Favourite authors   Children's: C. S. Lewis and Penelope Lively. Adults': Muriel Spark, Margaret Atwood, Anne Tyler.

Profession   Editor of teaching material.

Awards   Choysa Bursary for Children's Writers 1983.
NZ Library Association Esther Glen Award 1984 for *Elephant Rock*.
NZ Children's Book of the Year 1985 for *Visitors*.
Honor Prize, Australian Children's Book Award 1989 for *The Lake at the End of the World*.
Allan Marshall Prize for Children's Literature 1989 for *The Lake at the End of the World*.
Runner-up, Guardian Children's Fiction Award 1990 for *The Lake at the End of the World*.

Caroline Macdonald grew up in Taranaki as the youngest of four children. There was a large gap between her and the next one up in the family, and she remembers being alone a great deal, spending most of her time reading books, particularly the novels of C. S. Lewis. Perhaps that is why her own books, like those of C. S. Lewis, have a fantasy element and explore different time levels.

Time is very important in her first novel, *Elephant Rock*. It begins:

> Twenty years ago, when Mum was twelve, those waves were breaking against the very same rocks, and twenty years before that, and before that . . .
>
> They keep on going, she thought, on and on, the same way, century after century. The dry sand trickled between her fingers and slipped back into the usual hills and hollows.

But the sands of time are running out for Ann's mother, who is dying of cancer.

They are staying in the West Coast holiday house where the mother lived as a child. She used to swim out to Elephant Rock and one day, when Ann is doing the same, she feels that she is changing, going back to being her own mother twenty years earlier. Her experiences in her mother's past help her to come to terms with the present and to understand her mother's death better. It is a sad subject but it is never morbid. The point is made that Ann's mother had led the life she had wanted to and that it is more important to have quality than to have quantity of living.

Like Ann in *Elephant Rock*, Terry in *Visitors* is an only child. His parents are rich professional people who have little time for their son, although they give him expensive presents, such as a VCR on his birthday. It is when he is experimenting with this that he picks up unusual signals he cannot understand. They are from 'Visitors' from outer space who have been trapped in our world for hundreds of years because no one can understand their messages. There seems to be no solution to the puzzle until Terry is helped by the physically handicapped girl next door. Because the only way she can communicate is through a word processor, she is better able to understand what the Visitors are saying so that she and Terry can begin to help them escape to their own world.

An only child needs adults more than a child in a big family, but communicating with them is not always easy. Ann knows that soon she will no longer be able to talk with her mother, and Terry's parents have no time to talk to him. Another breakdown in communication occurs in *Yellow Boarding House*, in which a mother and daughter are stranded in Melbourne with no money. In *Joseph's Boat*, a long picture book for older children, Joseph's father fails to realise that his son is lonely on their remote island until Joseph takes a boat out by himself and is nearly lost at sea.

Caroline Macdonald is particularly interested in children who, for some reason, have grown up isolated from their own age group, from television and from rock music. In *The Lake at the End of the World* there are two such teenagers, who suddenly meet after having had totally different upbringings and never having seen anyone of their own age. The book takes place in the year 2025, after the planet has been almost killed by pollution. The only place where creatures and plants have survived is a lake in New Zealand. Quite unknown to one another, there are two groups of people close to the lake. The first is a very highly organised community, which has lived for some years entirely underground in caves. But one day one of its members, Hector, a teenager, finds his way above ground and meets Diana. She and her parents are the only survivors living on the shores of the lake, but they have no electricity and no modern labour-saving devices.

Hector and Diana argue fiercely at first, but when Diana's mother becomes ill they go down to the caves together in search of medicine. Events there force them to cooperate. They discover that the underground community is breaking down — what had started as an ideal, a Utopia, had become a nightmare, a Distopia, because the man who was once a wise leader had become a tyrant.

Like all good fantasy and science-fiction stories Caroline Macdonald's books work on different levels. The first, and most obvious, is the finely told story that keeps the pages turning because the reader simply must know what happens next. Then there are the carefully imagined settings, such as the one in *Visitors*:

> One wall of the sitting room was all glass. Outside there was the tiled terrace and beyond that the lawn with an old rhododendron tree in its centre. The rain fell steadily. The red tiles on the terrace were turned to a glistening black by the water lying on them. The only colours outside were shades of green: the grass, the rhododendron, the shrubs in the corner, the patch of native bush at the far end of the garden. Then the strange thing happened . . . The world outside the windows . . . became totally colourless.

The next level in her books is that of the characters and their relationships and finally there are all the other issues that interest Caroline Macdonald: the nature of time, scientific discoveries, communication and how people use power.

Central to *The Lake at the End of the World* is the problem of pollution and Caroline Macdonald says she is certainly a 'Greenie'. She supports Green politics because she really does think that the world is more likely to be destroyed by pollution than by nuclear war. Of course, any author's interests and concerns can be seen in their novels, but Caroline Macdonald is a very well-mannered writer. She never pushes her own opinions, but rather invites her readers to join her on a journey of exploration. Her gift for story telling and her elegant use of language make sure that it will be an enjoyable one.

BIBLIOGRAPHY

Elephant Rock. Hodder & Stoughton, Auckland, 1983.

Visitors. Hodder & Stoughton, Auckland, 1984.

Yellow Boarding House. OUP, Auckland, 1985.

Joseph's Boat. Illus. Chris Gaskin. Hodder & Stoughton, Auckland, 1988.

The Lake at the End of the World. Hodder & Stoughton, Auckland, 1988.

Earthgames. Shortland, Auckland, 1988.

The Seventh Head. Shortland, Auckland, 1988.

Act It Out (six one-act plays for secondary school ESL students). Canberra Curriculum Development Centre, Department of Employment, Education and Training, 1988.

Speaking to Miranda. Hodder & Stoughton, Auckland, 1990.

MARGARET MAHY

Born   Whakatane,
21 March 1936. She was
the eldest of five children
and now has grown-up
daughters of her own.
She lives in Governors
Bay, near Lyttelton.

Pets   A large variety over
the years, currently three
cats and a rabbit, Mrs
Gibbon.

Favourite food   Salads.

Favourite pastimes   Reading, listening to music
(especially J. S. Bach, Vivaldi, Mozart and Scott
Joplin), going to films, gardening and astronomy.

Favourite authors   Almost too many to name. As a
child she enjoyed R. L. Stevenson's *Treasure Island*
and Captain Marryat's books. As an adult she
numbers among her favourite authors for children
Eleanor Farjeon, Russell Hoban, Joan Aiken, Leon
Garfield, Rosemary Sutcliff, Helen Cresswell and
Diana Wynne Jones. She enjoys reading non-fiction
books on philosophy, astronomy and science.

Worries   She worries that people are reading less,
that they want the 'instant rewards' of television,
which needs less effort than choosing and reading a
book.

Awards   NZ Library Association Esther Glen Award,
in 1970 for *The Lion in the Meadow*, in 1972 for
The First Margaret Mahy Storybook, in 1983 for

The Haunting, and in 1985 for *The Changeover*.
NZ Literary Fund Grant 1976.
Italian Premier Grafico Award 1976 for *The Wind Between the Stars*.
Dutch Silver Pencil Award 1977 for *The Boy Who Was Followed Home*.
British Library Association Carnegie Medal, in 1983 for *The Haunting*, and in 1985 for *The Changeover*.
Observer Prize 1987 for *Memory*.

Margaret Mahy deserves a book to herself, and there is one, listed in the bibliography. She is not only the most famous children's writer in New Zealand but one of the most famous in the world. She has written books for all age groups, from pre-schoolers to near adult. Her work has been translated into more than a dozen languages and a glance at the awards she has won shows how much her stories are valued.

Many of us living in New Zealand have been lucky enough to meet Margaret Mahy. She loves visiting schools and often dresses up for the occasion, arriving as a penguin or a possum, or wearing a multi-coloured wig. She bubbles over with fun as she tells her stories. Even if she were not a first-class author she would be in demand as a splendid entertainer. But why do children and adults from around the world, who have never met her, enjoy her books as much as we do?

One reason is undoubtedly her sense of humour. So many of her stories are funny. Take 'The Wonderful Red "Memory" Stretch Wool Socks' (in *The Downhill Crocodile Whizz*). It begins: 'There was once a boy called Sam Snowgrass who had fine big feet for a boy his size . . . His father, on the other hand, had small dainty feet for a father his size.' When Sam's mother, who works in the Dinosaur Room of the Science Library, buys four pairs of bright red 'memory' stretch wool socks, which 'remember the shape of your feet', it is all too easy to get them muddled. One day Sam's father sets out for work and is carried by his feet past his own bus stop and on to Sam's school. He is, of course, wearing Sam's 'memory' socks. Meanwhile Sam is taken by his feet to his father's office . . .

Then there are stories like *The Great Piratical Rumbustification*, in which pirates form a baby-sitting agency, then take over the houses where they baby-sit for piratical parties that go 'like fireworks whizzing and buzzing and going off BANG — filling the air with rainbows and parrot feathers'.

Margaret Mahy's own love of parties and celebrations and, of course, the food that goes with them is reflected in several titles — *Chocolate Porridge, The Tick Tock Party, The Rare Spotted Birthday Party* — all of which show that birthdays are important. So important that not having one is the central theme for *The Birthday Burglar*. In this book Bassington is a lonely and bored boy who has only an elderly butler to care for him because his parents are always away. 'Something's missing from my life,' he says. 'I don't know what it is but I intend to find out.' Fortunately he has his own library and sets out to read about other children. At last he realises . . .

> 'I have all that the heart could desire, but I've never had a birthday. In these books birthdays seem to be special days that children look forward to. They have birthday cake and balloons . . . Why haven't I ever had a birthday? Where can I buy one?'

When he discovers that birthdays are not to be bought or sold he sets out to steal some . . .

One of Margaret Mahy's earliest birthday memories is of the time she was living with her parents in a caravan in Houhora in the far north, because her father was building a wharf there. She loved the caravan but it had no proper stove. How was her mother to bake a birthday cake for her fifth birthday? They were too far from the shops to buy one. But on her birthday morning a large parcel arrived from her Aunt Francie. In it were homemade biscuits iced with the letters of her name, a birthday cake and candles and other tins and packets of wonderful things to eat. She had been sent a party through the post!

Like Aunt Francie, kind adults in Margaret Mahy's books are splendid providers of food. Mr John Miller in *The Bus under the Leaves* is a very good cook whose kitchen is full of the aroma of cakes and bread. Mr Harrington in *Clancy's Cabin* thoughtfully arranges for bacon and egg pie and sausages on a camping holiday and in *The Pirate Uncle* the Pirate Uncle serves meals of a most mouthwatering kind: 'cherry cake and chicken eaten with fingers, fish, fresh caught . . . or sardines and homemade bread and salad'.

The uncle had a mysterious and possibly a pirate past, and Margaret Mahy is often asked why so many of her stories are about pirates. She thinks it may be because as a child she had been fascinated by pirates in the many swashbuckling adventures her father had read to her. She had always seen them as adventurous free spirits, rather like the pirate woman who longed to return to the sea in *The Man Whose Mother Was a Pirate*.

Mahy pirates are seldom really wicked. They are more bad mannered and inefficient than anything else. The ones in *The Pirates' Mixed-Up Voyage* have 'manners that were very low, but they made up for this by having their hopes very high'. They were always more interested in food than in navigation. Then there were those in *Sailor Jack and the Twenty Orphans*, who were a 'slouching grubby lot, and though they were brave and bold at fighting with swords the thought of soap and water made them turn pale as cheese'.

Not all Margaret's pirates are quite what they seem, especially the older ones in *The Great Piratical Rumbustification*, who have returned from the sea to 'live on their ill-gotten riches'. When they are not wearing their pirate clothes they appear 'as ordinary grey-haired distinguished lawyers and business men', and when neighbours and passers-by have changed hats with them 'you could not tell one from the other unless you looked closely, and not always then'. She makes us wonder who are the real pirates in society.

If Margaret Mahy's pirates are not entirely bad, neither are her witches. After all, she herself grew up with the nickname of 'The Witch', given her after she had gone to a fancy-dress party dressed as one. (She had wanted to be a fairy but her mother thought she looked more like a witch!) She sees her witches and wizards as forms of energy, which whirl people around and leave them never quite the same again. They often suggest that there is more to the world than meets the eye, and they give her stories those different levels of meaning that make them so memorable.

It is the witches and wizards who introduce elements of magic, and that word 'magic' can mean many things. In her novel *The Haunting*, for instance, it could mean 'imagination', or 'creativity'. When she was young the old grandmother discovered that she was a magician (not a witch), but she did not want to be. She set out to order and tidy everything, 'to crush the magic right out of her life, to wipe out her own specialness . . . She put a false order on things around her.' She was not going to allow her imagination or creativity to bubble up in case it might lead her in different directions, away from the ordinary and the comfortable.

Magic is often a name given over the years to something that is not understood. If Stone Age people came back today they would think that we were magicians; we have moving pictures to show us happenings from afar (television), we can fly (in aeroplanes), we can talk to people thousands of miles away (by telephone). Perhaps magic and science are not so very different from each other.

Margaret Mahy is certainly interested in science — particularly in astronomy. One of the first things you see when you enter her unusual house in Governors Bay is a little balcony with a telescope for star watching. One of the characters in a novel for young adults, *The Catalogue of the Universe*, is called Tycho, after Tycho Brahe, a famous Danish astronomer of the seventeenth century, who built one of the first observatories in the Western World.

Raging Robots and Unruly Uncles is a more light-hearted novel about technology rather than serious science. Two sets of cousins construct robots to send as presents to one another. Prudence, a well brought-up girl, makes her robot, the Nadger, from 'spare radio parts, biscuit tins and old soup cans, milk bottle tops, bent nails, wire and an old frying pan'. When switched off its needle points to 'Perfect Virtue', but when the batteries are working the wickedness circuits are activated and 'the needle crept round from CARELESS to DOWNRIGHT INCONSIDERATE on to BAD, to VILLAINOUS and finally to SUPERVILLAINOUS and then the robot behaved like a perfect demon'. It causes consternation in the household of her six boy cousins who had sent her quite a mild, well-behaved robot, Lilly Rose Blossom, who is much too good to be true . . .

So far Margaret Mahy has written only one science-fiction novel, *Aliens in the Family*, in which librarians on the planet of Galgonqua are cataloguing the universe and send a student, Bond, to the planet of his ancestors to check up on life in this world. He discovers a great deal about human relationships and during the course of the novel the family who befriend him go back in time to witness the huge volcanic eruption that created Lyttelton Harbour millions of years ago.

Earthquakes or volcanic eruptions occur in a surprising number of books. They give a clue to her childhood in Whakatane, not far from the active volcano White Island and where they frequently felt earth tremors. In spite of all these New Zealand 'clues', when she first started writing publishers turned down her stories because they did not have sufficient New Zealand content, although the *School Journal* did accept a number. At the time, in the late 1960s, people wanted books with a local flavour, about the Maori, or early settlers, or adventures in the bush. Margaret Mahy's stories about pirates, witches and wizards were thought to be too 'English'.

It was a chance breakthrough that set her on the path to fame. The *School Journal* sent an exhibition to the USA, and there they were seen by an editor, Sarah Chockla Gross. As soon as she read Margaret Mahy's stories she realised that they would make wonderful picture books. She rang Helen Hoke Watts, children's editor of Franklin Watts publishing house, and read them to her over the phone. Mrs Watts was equally enthusiastic and in 1969 five of Margaret's stories, including *A Lion in the Meadow,* were published in New York.

Margaret Mahy's more recent novels for older readers have been very recognisably set in Governors Bay or Christchurch. One of these is *Memory*, which tells how a teenage boy forms a friendship with a strange old lady, Sophie. Sophie suffers from Alzheimer's Disease, a cruel illness that gradually destroys brain cells so that people lose their memories. The warm, vivid picture given of Sophie is undoubtedly based on old Aunt Francie, the one who had sent the birthday party by post. In her later years she lived next door to Margaret Mahy in Governors Bay and had almost totally lost her memory.

Margaret was very fond of Aunt Francie and tells an amusing story of how, although most of the time her forgetfulness was very inconvenient, there was one occasion when it was most useful. This was when she had been told over the phone that her novel *The Haunting* had won the Carnegie Medal, given for the best children's book in the English-speaking world. But there was a snag. She had been told early because she had to book her passage to London to receive the medal, but it was to be an absolute secret. Absolutely no one must be told.

She was simply bursting to tell someone and then it occurred to her that Aunt Francie, who could never remember anything from one minute to the next, would never repeat it. So it was that every day she went next door and said, 'Aunty, isn't it marvellous, I've won the Carnegie Medal.' And every day her aunt replied, 'Have you, dear, isn't that splendid!'

Margaret Mahy has always been interested in old people. When she left school she thought she might like to be a nurse and worked on wards for the aged in the local hospital. Several of her books give a very sympathetic picture of the elderly. In her poetic story *The Wind Between the Stars* she contrasts two old ladies, Miss Gibb, who only thinks about the past, and the fine dresses she once wore, and poor old shuffling Phoebe, whose husband has died and whose children have left home. Yet Phoebe feels no different from when she was young. 'I'm still the same,' she says. 'Here I am . . . But who is there to remember me? Who is there left to call me by my name . . . to know who I really am and to see the real me looking out from behind all these wrinkles?' But Phoebe can still dance and is willing to join the lions, mermaids and princesses in the procession that goes with the wind from between the stars, which takes them, 'as it takes all things that flow and are free . . . and if anyone wants to go with it, it will take them, but they mustn't hope to come back again.'

Great-Uncle Magnus Pringle in *The Ultra-Violet Catastrophe* is another old person who is much more interesting than he at first appears. He resents being treated like a pot plant and is very happy to paddle in mud with his great-niece Sally or to use exciting words like 'ultra-violet catastrophe' or 'seismological singularity' to relieve the boredom. In a recent picture book, *Making Friends*, an elderly couple are helped by their dogs to make friends and become less lonely.

Margaret Mahy enjoyed working with old people but she did not enjoy other aspects of nursing. She longed to spend more time talking with patients and less on jobs such as making beds. So she decided to leave nursing and go to Auckland University, where she studied English, history, French, education and philosophy. Philosophy is really a study of ideas and her enquiring mind is always asking questions. Why are we here? What is the purpose of life? Do we have a free choice in what we do or are we part of a plan?

There are amusing echoes of these questions in the novel *The Pirates' Mixed-Up Voyage*, in which a parrot, named Toothpick, cries, 'Doom and Destiny', for 'he was a Determinist and believed that everything happening in the Universe was part of a Vast Mysterious Plan'. But his owner, Lionel Wafer, believes in Free Will. 'What rubbish, Toothpick!' he would cry. 'The World isn't run according to any Plan and that's that. In the heroic life things are simple, free and unplanned.' Lionel Wafer is a pirate, however, and it has to be said that the pirates' mixed-up voyage is fairly simple, moderately free and most certainly unplanned!

From university Margaret Mahy went to library school and then worked as a librarian in Wellington and in Christchurch. One way and another libraries feature in a number of her books, one of the best loved being *The Librarian and the Robbers*. The librarian, Serena Laburnum, is kidnapped by robbers, but when they all catch the 'raging measles' she is shocked to discover that these villains are almost illiterate. They have not read a thing. 'Very well,' says Miss Laburnum. 'We shall start with Peter Rabbit and work our way up from there.' Like all good librarians, Serena is careful about who may borrow books and about shelving them, so after she has returned to the library and the robber chief, Salvation Loveday, is fleeing from the police, she carefully stamps him with a number and files him under L.

Margaret Mahy is frequently asked where her ideas come from, and she answers that they come from her everyday surroundings. With an imagination as lively as hers, any ordinary event can spark off a story. For instance, she once parked by a parking meter and noticed that it was standing with others in a row, in grass. Most people would probably not even have noticed this, but it set her wondering. Other parking meters she had seen were set in concrete. How had these come to be in grass? Had they been planted there? Had they started out as a packet of parking meter seeds, which some head gardener had sown? Did they come up with their heads bent and slowly straighten?

Margaret Mahy believes that imagination 'is the ability to deal creatively with reality'. A story that exemplifies this is 'Thunderstorms and Rainbows' (in *The Downhill Crocodile Whizz*). It is about a town called Trickle, 'a babbling, bubbling, swishing, swashing, murmuring, meandering kind of a town'. But Trickle has a problem . . . it is the rainiest town in the world. The townsfolk are very sensitive to unkind remarks about their climate and their only solution is to arrest any visitor who dares to get off the ferry and say, 'Goodness, it *does* rain here, doesn't it!' Then a young man arrives who says, 'I think that you have been telling people the wrong things about Trickle . . . Suppose you were to invite people to come especially *because* of the rain.' He really does 'deal creatively with reality' and turns failure into success.

We have looked at many reasons for Margaret Mahy's success: her humour, her love of celebrations, her use of magic and her compassion. But however interesting the subject matter, her stories and novels would not have won fame if they had not been well written. She loves playing with words; her delight in language enables her to create memorable names like Mrs Discombobulous or Terrible Crabmeat, or exclamations such as 'Great Whillping Gradgenuzzlers!'. It leads her to write descriptive passages like the one in *The Man Whose Mother Was a Pirate* when the little man first sees the sea.

> He hadn't thought it would roll like kettledrums and swish itself onto the beach. He opened his mouth and the drift and the dream of it, the weave and the wave of it, the fume and the foam of it, never left him again.

Her command of language means that she can adapt it for

different age groups or for television. Her writing in stories and novels for older readers is more terse and economical. In 'The Devil and the Corner Grocer' (from *The Chewing-Gum Rescue*), a strange Traveller appears.

The little grocery was warm with its hissing heater and yellow electric lights yet suddenly the lights dimmed threateningly while the heater went dark and silent. The corner grocery became as cold as a wicked wish. Mr Philpott knew who was there . . . the Traveller stood before him, meeting his gaze with a savage smile. It was as if he had slashed at him with a razor of ice.

Margaret Mahy continues to write beginner readers, picture books for younger children and short stories for older ones, and has now published four 'young adult' novels, but it is difficult to predict where her interests will next take her. She has adapted stories and novels for television as well as writing original television serials. She has enjoyed the experience of working in studios but it is difficult to imagine that the restrictions of television will ever totally satisfy her. Like so many of her own characters, she is an adventurous free spirit. In one of her most recent stories, 'The Bridge Builder' (from *The Door in the Air*), she draws on memories of her own father, who was a bridge builder. She is like Merlin, the Bridge Builder's son, who says:

'I am a traveller, crossing all the bridges my father has built . . . Someday I shall become a journey, winding over hills, across cities, along sea shores and through shrouded forests, crossing my father's bridges and the bridges of other men, as well as all the infinitely divided roads and splintered pathways that lie between them.'

BIBLIOGRAPHY

Books for children

Picture books

The Dragon of an Ordinary Family. Illus. Helen Oxenbury. Heinemann, London, 1969.

A Lion in the Meadow. Illus. Jenny Williams. Dent, London, 1969.

Mrs Discombobulous. Illus. Jan Brychta. Dent, London, 1969.

Pillycock's Shop. Illus. Carol Barker. Dobson, London, 1969.

The Procession. Illus. Charles Mozley. Dent, London, 1969.

The Little Witch. Illus. Charles Mozley. Dent, London, 1970.

Sailor Jack and the Twenty Orphans. Illus. Robert Bartelt. Dent, London, 1970.

The Princess and the Clown. Illus. Carol Barker. Dobson, London, 1971.

The Boy with Two Shadows. Illus. Jenny Williams. Dent, London, 1971.

The Man Whose Mother Was a Pirate. Illus. Brian Froud. Dent, London, 1972.

The Railway Engine and the Hairy Brigands. Illus. Brian Froud. Dent, London, 1973.

Rooms to Let. Illus. Jenny Williams. Dent, London, 1975.

The Witch in the Cherry Tree. Dent, London, 1974.

The Rare Spotted Birthday Party. Illus. Belinda Lyon. Watts, London, 1974.

Stepmother. Illus. Terry Burton. Watts, London, 1974.

The Ultra-Violet Catastrophe. Illus. Brian Froud. Dent, London, 1975.

The Great Millionaire Kidnap. Illus. Jan Brychta. Dent, London, 1975.

The Wind Between the Stars. Illus. Brian Froud. Dent, London, 1976.

David's Witch Doctor. Illus. Jim Russell. Watts, London, 1976.

Leaf Magic. Illus. Jenny Williams. Dent, London, 1976.

The Boy Who Was Followed Home. Illus. Stephen Kellogg. Dent, London, 1977.

Jam. Illus. Helen Craig. Dent, London, 1985.

The Great White Man-Eating Shark. Illus. Jonathan Allen. Dent, London, 1989.

Making Friends. Illus. Wendy Smith. Dent, London, 1990.

Pumpkin Man and the Crafty Creeper. Illus. Helen Craig. Cape, London, 1990.

The Seven Chinese Brothers. Illus. Jean and Mou-sien Tseng. Scholastic, New York, 1990.

Collections of stories

The First Margaret Mahy Story Book. Illus. Shirley Hughes. Dent, London, 1972.

The Second Margaret Mahy Story Book. Illus. Shirley Hughes. Dent, London, 1973.

The Third Margaret Mahy Story Book. Illus. Shirley Hughes. Dent, London, 1975.

A Lion in the Meadow and Five Other Favourites. Illus. Jenny Williams. Dent, London, 1976.

Nonstop Nonsense. Illus. Quentin Blake. Dent, London, 1977.

The Great Piratical Rumbustification and The Librarian and the Robbers. Illus. Quentin Blake. Dent, London, 1978.

The Chewing-Gum Rescue and Other Stories. Illus. Jan Ormerod. Dent, London, 1982.

Leaf Magic and Five Other Favourites. Illus. Margaret Chamberlain. Dent, London, 1984.

The Birthday Burglar and A Very Wicked Headmistress. Illus. Margaret Chamberlain. Dent, London, 1984.

The Downhill Crocodile Whizz and Other Stories. Illus. Ian Newsham. Dent, London, 1986.

Mahy Magic. Illus. Shirley Hughes. Dent, London, 1986.

The Horrible Story and Others. Illus. Shirley Hughes. Dent, London, 1987.

The Door in the Air and Other Stories. Illus. Diana Catchpole. Dent, London, 1988.

Junior novels
Clancy's Cabin. Illus. Trevor Stubley. Dent, London, 1974.
The Bus under the Leaves. Illus. Margery Gill. Dent, London, 1975.
The Pirate Uncle. Illus. Mary Dinsdale. Dent, London, 1977.
Raging Robots and Unruly Uncles. Illus. Peter Stevenson. Dent, London, 1981.
The Pirates' Mixed-up Voyage. Illus. Margaret Chamberlain. Dent, London, 1983.
The Blood and Thunder Adventure on Hurricane Peak. Illus. Wendy Smith. Dent, London, 1989.

Novels for older readers
The Haunting. Dent, London, 1982.
The Changeover. Dent, London, 1984.
The Catalogue of the Universe. Dent, London, 1985.
Aliens in the Family. Ashton Scholastic and Reed Methuen, Auckland, 1986.
The Tricksters. Dent, London, 1986.
Memory. Dent, London, 1987.

Readers
5 Story Chest Books for Shortland, Auckland, 1982.
15 Sunshine Books for Heinemann, Auckland, 1986.
8 readers for Department of Education School Publications Branch, Wellington, 1982–85.
32 readers for Shortland, Auckland, 1984–88.
20 readers for Heinemann, Auckland, 1986–87.

Poetry
Seventeen Kings and Forty-two Elephants. Illus. Charles Mozley. Dent, London, 1972.
The Tin Can Band and Other Poems. Illus. Honey de Lacey. Dent, London, 1989.

Non-fiction
Look Under 'V'. Illus. Deirdre Gardner. Department of Education, Wellington, 1977.

A biography written for children
Introducing Margaret Mahy (by Betty Gilderdale). Viking, Auckland, 1987.

Books for adults
New Zealand Yesterday and Today. Watts, London, 1975.

JOANNA ORWIN

Born   Nelson, 28 November 1944. She has three children and she lives in Christchurch.

Pets   Two cats, Tinker and Moppet.

Favourite food   Granny Smith apples.

Favourite pastimes   Reading, tramping, gardening, sailing, rowing and art.

Favourite authors   Children's: Rosemary Sutcliff and Henry Treece.

Profession   Scientist. Before she married she worked as a plant ecologist with the Forest and Range Experiment Station at Rangiora. She now edits scientific articles for the Forest Research Institute, based at the University of Canterbury.

Awards   NZ Children's Book of the Year 1986 for *The Guardian of the Land*.

When Joanna Orwin visited England in 1975 she was fascinated by the old buildings. She spent fifteen months in Cambridge, where her husband was working, and knew that almost every stone could tell a story. But even before the beautiful city had been built 700 years ago, people had lived in the countryside there. Britain, like New Zealand, had had many invaders. The Celts, the Romans, the Anglo-Saxons and the Normans had come in succession. How could she find out about them?

She turned to the novels of Rosemary Sutcliff and found

that the distant past of Britain came alive. Not only were they wonderful stories to read, they left her knowing a great deal more about the people who had lived so long ago. She wished that there were books like Rosemary Sutcliff's about New Zealand.

By comparison, when they returned to New Zealand, the land seemed empty, without any sense of what had happened in the past. Yet a great deal *must* have happened! People had lived here and wherever there are people there is a story. How far would those stories have been shaped by the land, by the mountains, rivers, lakes and bush? she wondered.

The landforms of New Zealand had fascinated Joanna Orwin from the time she first went tramping with her two sisters and their doctor father around Lake Rotoiti. She decided to study geography and botany at the University of Canterbury, although her prizes at Nelson Girls' College had been for poetry and essay writing.

So when she started thinking about New Zealand's past she thought of it in terms of the landscape she knew so well, in the north of the South Island. By now her two older children were at school and the youngest was sleeping during the day, so she had time to think about writing a novel. Like Rosemary Sutcliff, she did careful research, and she found that the first people to live in this land were the moa hunters. She knew that moa hunters went on summer wanderings to hunt birds, and she knew that they must have needed weapons for hunting. But where did they get the stone?

Because she had studied geology she knew that there had been argillite (pakohe or mudstone) quarries between Nelson and Blenheim. Although it is not as hard as greenstone, argillite is easier to flake and turn into adzes — easier, too, for a boy to carve. What if there had once lived a boy who was not very interested in hunting moa but who was very good at carving? This was the idea behind her first novel, *Ihaka and the Summer Wandering*, which was followed by *Ihaka and the Prophecy*.

Both are set in Delaware Bay, near Nelson, an area Joanna Orwin remembers from her childhood as a wild, magical place. By the end of the first book Ihaka has discovered his ability to carve stone. In the second he is apprenticed to a tohunga to learn the craft of shaping stone and wood. He needs all his skills because his tribe has decided to journey across Cook Strait. This means making a much larger ocean-going canoe, stronger than the ones they use for offshore fishing. The book shows first the choosing then the felling of a giant totara, which has to be fashioned into a great canoe. Because they have only stone tools this takes a great deal of time.

As though in keeping with the times of Ihaka, Joanna Orwin does not hurry with her story. These are not fast-moving adventures, but they do help the reader to experience the atmosphere of the period and how it must have felt to live in Ihaka's world. After reading them visits to museums will come alive through understanding something of the people who built canoes of such beauty in spite of great hardship.

Another place that intrigued Joanna Orwin was Kaikoura, an area important both to the early moa hunters and to European settlers. The first intact moa's egg to be found was discovered there, there are fine limestone caves, seals bask on beaches, and the fishing is excellent. Above all, whales visit the bays and the area became famous for its whaling. How exciting it would be, she thought, to slip back in time in Kaikoura.

So began *The Guardian of the Land*, in which a modern boy, David, is sent to stay in Kaikoura with relatives. He becomes friends with a Maori boy, Rua, whose grandmother, Nanny Henare, is very anxious to recover a family heirloom before she dies. It is a whalebone pendant, called the Guardian of the Land. As they become more sensitive to the land David and Rua experience a series of flashbacks into the past. They join a seal hunt, watch a raid on a pa and sail with the whalers. Each episode leads them closer to the discovery of the pendant.

What happens in the past is always there, trapped in the land. Perhaps ghosts from the past are still watching present-day happenings? Would it be possible for our actions in the present to alter anything that happened in the past? These are the questions behind Joanna Orwin's latest novel, *The Watcher in the Forest*. This is set in another place she knows well, the earthquake-torn landscape between Murchison and Lewis Pass. Three present-day children, two teenagers and a younger sister, set off on a carefully planned tramp in the bush, but whenever they stop, Jen, the middle one, is aware of being watched. Gradually the others become drawn into her experiences. They realise that the spirit of a long-dead Maori is wanting them to return a valuable piece of greenstone to the burial chamber of a man who had been murdered. This means going back into the past — but will they ever get back to their own time . . . ?

So far Joanna Orwin has written only four novels, because all of them have taken so long to research. But she enjoyed doing this. Visits to Kaikoura and to museums became family outings. Going to an archaeological dig at Kaikoura was wonderful, because it provided background information for *The Guardian of the Land*. The land is perhaps the most important factor in Joanna Orwin's novels, because it is what gives New Zealand its very special character. Like Jen in *The Watcher in the Forest*, she knows that 'the land gave of itself to people and that gift bound together those who came after and those who had gone before . . . Jen understood what the Watcher had told her, "Men come, men depart. The land alone endures."'

BIBLIOGRAPHY

Ihaka and the Summer Wandering. OUP, Auckland, 1983.
Ihaka and the Prophecy. OUP, Auckland, 1984.
The Guardian of the Land. OUP, Auckland, 1985.
Watcher in the Forest. OUP, Auckland, 1987.

EVE SUTTON

Born Preston, England, 14 September 1906. She has two sons, and lives in Auckland.

Pets No pet at present, but usually cats.

Favourite food Avocados.

Favourite pastimes Reading and golf.

Favourite authors As a child: Henty and Rudyard Kipling. As an adult: E. M. Forster.

Dislikes Loud pop music. She also worries about poor grammar and slovenly writing.

Profession A teacher before coming to New Zealand.

Awards NZ Library Association Esther Glen Award 1975 for *My Cat Likes to Hide in Boxes*. Children's Literature Association Award 1990 for an outstanding contribution to NZ children's literature.

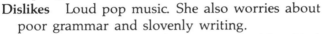

Eve Sutton says, 'It never crossed my mind when, as a child, I was reading every book I could get hold of, that somebody, some actual person, had sat down and written them . . . The first glimpse I had was when somebody said, "Have you read Henty's tales?" Never heard of him. So I went to the library and asked, "Have you any Hentist Tales?" The librarian looked rather puzzled but suddenly brightened. "Ah yes, you mean Henty. Come along." And they found me a book by Henty and that taught me just in that one flash that somebody called Henty had written that book.'

By the time she was at secondary school she had discovered the stories and poems of Rudyard Kipling, so when there was a competition for the school magazine to write a parody of a well-known poem she chose to do a different version of Kipling's 'If'. She says, 'I was passionately keen on hockey so I wrote a hockey poem. It began, "If you could hit the ball when all about you are missing it and always giving stick . . . "' She won the competition and had to walk the full length of the hall to get her prize while everyone clapped.

She continues, 'Anyway that set me off thinking perhaps I wouldn't mind writing. Just for a tenth of a second . . . then the whole thing went from my mind. I was too busy enjoying life, far too busy playing hockey, sitting exams and so on. All school was absolute bliss. I didn't do anything in writing except work occasionally for the school magazine. And then life went on and right into middle age until I had two schoolboy sons and we came out here to New Zealand.'

She was still not thinking about becoming an author until a friend of hers told her that she had written an article for a magazine and it had been published. Not to be outdone, Eve Sutton thought she would try to write an article. She was very interested in the blind and in how they could read using the Braille alphabet, so she wrote about Braille. To her great joy the article was accepted. 'This is easy,' she thought. 'I'm a natural author! Now don't tell people how easy it is or they'll all be doing it. So I sent some more articles off. Well, of course, you know what happened to them — they hardly even touched the editor's desk before they were back again.'

So, she thought, 'Woman, you don't know the first thing about writing.' Then she saw a handout from Tamaki College, listing night-school classes for the year. And there in the middle of the list was journalism. 'We learned about beginnings and endings, short sentences, short words, brevity, grab your reader in the very first paragraph. Do your market research, most essential. Decide who you are writing for and write for them.'

By this time Eve Sutton had taken up playing golf — not quite as strenuous as hockey — and had just got her first handicap. On the journalism course they had to write one article every week, so she decided to write one on golf. She says, 'I had the absolute cheek to write an article for a men's magazine on how to putt and I sent the article off to an English golf magazine.' To her astonishment the magazine accepted it and even paid her. By now her sons were grown up and she had more spare time, so she joined the Women Writers group, and entered a short story competition and won! The story was published in the *New Zealand Woman*.

It had never occurred to Eve Sutton to write for children. That idea was put into her head one sunny afternoon when she was back in England, visiting friends and family. The wife of a younger cousin from New Zealand was also visiting. She was an artist and as they sat in the garden enjoying the sunshine she said to Eve, 'Wouldn't it be fun to do a children's book together! You do the words and I'll do the pictures.'

The cousin's wife was Lynley Dodd and the picture book they did together was *My Cat Likes to Hide in Boxes*. It has become one of the most famous New Zealand picture books and it was the beginning of a career for both of them, although they did not work together again. Lynley Dodd went on to write and illustrate her own picture books for younger children. Her Hairy Maclary series is the best known. But Eve Sutton wanted to write adventure stories for older readers and she decided to set her novels in the past.

She and her family were immigrants to New Zealand, so she knew how hard it was to leave one country and come to another. It is difficult enough today when newcomers find a civilised country with houses, roads and transport. What must it have been like for the early settlers? she wondered. What would it have been like if you were a boy on your own?

The result of these questions was her first novel, *Green Gold*. It is quite short and tells how eleven-year-old Adam Sterling and his father set out for New Zealand to join an uncle here. But the father dies on the voyage, as so many people did on those crowded ships. That is bad enough, but when the ship docks in Auckland there is no sign of the uncle. Adam's dreadful first days on his own in a rough city are made even more exciting because he is in charge of treasure that his father had sent to the uncle and which Adam constantly fears may be stolen. He has no idea what the treasure is, and neither have we until the surprise ending.

Another boy on his own in early Auckland is Tuppenny Brown, in the book of that name. He has a difficult time because, like Charlie Blackiston in Margaret Beames's *The Parkhurst Boys*, Tuppenny has been in Parkhurst Prison. He had been put in prison in England for picking pockets but had been given a chance to come to New Zealand to start a new life. He really wants to turn over a new leaf. The trouble is that a bigger, older Parkhurst boy, Jake, is trying to bully him back into his old ways.

In *Johnny Sweep*, another young boy, Johnny, has signed on as a ship's cook on a whaling boat. He never dreamed he would be expected to cut up the whales and help in melting down the blubber. He so hates this messy, smelly job and the bullying ship's captain that he jumps ship in Auckland and makes his way to the gum fields, where he hopes to find work.

Eve Sutton says she learned a great deal about research while she was writing these books. Every detail has to be just right. For instance, in *Tuppenny Brown*, which is set in 1842, she had planned to have her settlers farm near Auckland, having cleared the kauri forest at Tamaki. 'That won't do,' said a friend. 'Rangitoto had erupted not long since and killed all the vegetation. There wouldn't have been any kauri forest at Tamaki.' So Eve Sutton decided to have the farm in New Lynn instead, that is until she showed the story to a librarian. 'No, this won't do,' said the librarian. 'Your story is set in 1842 and New Lynn wasn't opened up until 1843.' She had learned her lesson. Now, before she plans or writes a book she does every scrap of research first.

Green Gold, Tuppenny Brown and *Johnny Sweep* are all quite short books and are very easily read. But Eve Sutton had become enthusiastic about New Zealand's past, including the pre-European past. She set her longer novel, *Moa Hunter*, in the South Island, where the young hero Kotiri is a chief's son in a moa-hunting tribe. Catching the great birds is very difficult — one kick from their powerful legs could cause considerable damage. The moa hunters have to be carefully trained. But one day when Kotiri sees a moa he feels sure he can catch it, although his training is by no means complete. As a result he is kicked and so badly hurt that, although he recovers, he knows he will never be able to follow his father as chief of the tribe. The whole affair is made worse by knowing that it was his own fault, but by the book's end he has found something else to do that makes his life worthwhile.

Eve Sutton came back to early European settlers in a later book, *Surgeon's Boy*. The surgeon's boy, Jamie, is the son of a doctor who comes out to New Zealand after his wife has died. It proves to be an exciting journey. In Sydney, convicts hijack the boat and take it to the tough town of Kororareka (Russell) in the north, then down the coast to Port Nicholson, now Wellington.

By now Eve Sutton was knowledgeable about ships and convicts. She discovered something few people know about — that Pacific Islanders were taken to work as slaves in the sugar plantations of Queensland. The slave traders were called 'blackbirders' and in *Kidnapped by Blackbirders* she describes how they pretended to be missionaries so that the Islanders trusted them. They would then entice the Islanders on board ship and take them to Australia to work hard in cruel conditions. The book's hero, Paul, and his father are honest traders and, although they are English, they have black hair and tanned faces. So when Paul is kidnapped by blackbirders who think he is an Islander, they do not realise that he can understand them. By the time they reach Australia he has enough evidence to convict them and put an end to the wicked practice.

Eve Sutton's own favourite of her books is the latest, *Valley of Heavenly Gold*. It came about as the result of a holiday in the South Island, when she became interested in the nineteenth-century Otago gold rush. She tells how the young hero, Matthew, longs to accompany his father to the gold diggings but has to stay home with his mother and three sisters to mind the family shop. But when his father is brought home ill, Matthew and a Chinese friend go to the gold fields to collect the gold his father has left behind. Matthew's adventures at the diggings and his friendship with Chinese settlers make this an unusual story, and, as in a number of Eve Sutton's books, there is a surprise ending.

It may seem strange that a woman writer has chosen young men for her main characters. The fact of the matter is that in the last century girls were much more protected and would have been unlikely to have adventures in the rough, tough world of whaling, gum digging, gold mining and convict ships. Yet these are the sorts of adventures that interest Eve Sutton. It must also be remembered that her own children were boys and she was used to them and their friends and the sort of stories they liked to read.

She did write one book that was about neither cats nor boys, but about a girl and a dog! In *Skip for the Huntaway*, Skip is a pet collie dog given to Katie when her twin brothers were born. But when Katie goes to boarding school the badly trained Skip starts chasing chickens. Katie's farmer parents fear he might begin chasing sheep and the book opens with her father telling her that Skip must be sent away. That problem is overcome, only to be followed by one that is even worse . . . It is a story full of ups and downs, and has a surprising, but satisfying, ending.

Few people can have begun their career at the age of sixty-seven, as Eve Sutton did. Her most recent book was published when she was eighty-one. She is proof that growing old does not mean losing a sense of fun or of purpose. Through her reading and research and then through her imagination she has taken herself and her readers on some splendid, well-written adventures.

BIBLIOGRAPHY

My Cat Likes to Hide in Boxes. Illus. Lynley Dodd. Hamish Hamilton, London, 1973.

Green Gold. Hamish Hamilton, London, 1976.

Tuppenny Brown. Hamish Hamilton, London, 1977.

Johnny Sweep. Hamish Hamilton, London, 1977.

Moa Hunter. Hamish Hamilton, London, 1978.

Skip for the Huntaway. Price Milburn, Wellington, 1983.

Surgeon's Boy. Mallinson Rendel, Wellington, 1983.

Kidnapped by Blackbirders. Mallinson Rendel, Wellington, 1984.

Valley of Heavenly Gold. Mallinson Rendel, Wellington, 1987.

WILLIAM TAYLOR

Born   Wellington, 11 October 1938. He was the eldest of four children and has two grown-up sons of his own. He lives in Raurimu.

Favourite food   Almost everything. He cannot imagine why he is so thin!

Favourite pastimes   Outdoor pursuits such as gardening and walking. He likes meeting people, especially if they have a sense of humour.

Profession   Teacher.

Awards   Choysa Bursary for Children's Writers 1985.

Carrots do not appear in William Taylor's list of favourite foods, but they seem to have played an important part in his life. For one thing, he was for many years Mayor of the North Island carrot-growing town of Ohakune. He says he is one of the few people in the world to have unveiled a ten-metre-high replica of a carrot.

The vegetable also provided a turning point in William Taylor's career as a writer. During the 1970s he had written six novels for adults but then, in 1976, he wrote an amusing account of his experiences as a teacher, particularly on a school camp. He described vividly how one boy had taken his dinner to a helper, complaining that there was something black in it. 'It's burnt carrot,' said the helper. 'But burnt carrots don't have legs!' answered the boy, as he fished out a fly. So William Taylor gave the book one of the world's most original titles, *Burnt Carrots Don't Have Legs*. It was not written for children, but he realised that his own experiences in schools would be suitable for children's stories and from then on he ceased to write for adults.

One of the most enjoyable things about being a primary school teacher is the variety of jobs to be done. As well as work in the classroom there are school camps, sport, music and drama. William Taylor particularly enjoys producing plays and pantomimes. Once he produced *Snow White and the Seven Dwarfs* with twenty-seven dwarfs instead of seven. This was not because he could not count but because he felt sorry for all the people who wanted to act but for whom there were no parts. The easiest thing seemed to be to let them all be dwarfs. 'Why stop at seven?' he asked.

He used this particular episode in his book *Break a Leg*, the second in the series that begins with *The Worst Soccer Team Ever* and finishes with *Making Big Bucks*. All of them feature the imaginary (but very recognisable) characters of Greenhill Intermediate School — teachers, parents and, of course, children. One of the most memorable characters is Lavender Gibson, who is determined not to be disadvantaged in life because she is a girl. In one of the funniest scenes in New Zealand children's literature, she insists that she wants to play soccer, not netball. She is supported by her friends, two of whom are boys called Tom Coleman and Bogdan Lupescu. The fact that Lavender's and Bogdan's names are shortened to Lav and Bog is, William Taylor smiles, pure coincidence.

The Worst Soccer Team Ever and *Break a Leg* were adapted for television in a series called 'All for One' and William Taylor was astonished to see his imaginary characters come to life. 'It was a surreal and unforgettable experience for me on the final day of filming to stand and be photographed with the soccer team that had previously existed only in my mind.'

The three books about Greenhill Intermediate are amusing accounts of day-to-day life in and out of school, but William Taylor does more than simply entertain his readers. Like Lavender Gibson he really dislikes sexism and racism and, like the Greenhill Intermediate teachers, he believes that drama and sport help people learn to work together and make friends.

Teaching in small towns has meant that he gets to know parents and children very well, so that he sees the sad as well as the funny side of life. He knows only too well that people who have lived in the same place for many years can be unkind to newcomers. His first novel for children — and still his own favourite — *Pack Up, Pick Up and Off,* is based on something that really happened in one of the country schools where he worked. In it the children of a rabbiter's family suffer because the local people are suspicious of them simply because they have moved so often.

Animals play an important part in comforting children in two of his novels. *My Summer of the Lions* is his only book to be set in a big city — Wellington. In it he describes thirteen-year-old Malcolm Smith's unhappiness after his mother's death from cancer. His father is just as unhappy, but because they are both so wrapped up in their own misery they are unable to comfort each other. Malcolm takes to confiding in two elderly lions at the zoo, who turn out to be very good listeners!

The plight of a young possum leads to a very surprising friendship between Rosie and Michael in *Possum Perkins*. It is surprising because Rosie is a quiet, studious, only child, while Michael comes from a big, boisterous family and is more interested in football than in reading. But through helping Rosie to care for a young possum he realises that something is wrong at her home and his own warm-hearted mother becomes a great help to Rosie in her difficulties. William Taylor says he often thinks that Rosie and Michael are two sides of his own character. One part of him, like Rosie, enjoys being quiet and alone, but then there is the Michael side, which loves to be in the company of other people.

Perhaps he was feeling like having someone to talk to one day when he was driving in the Bay of Plenty. He picked up a hitch-hiker who, as they drove along, told him the story that he used as the basis for his novel *Shooting Through*. It starts with the escape of two boys from a remand home. They find their way to the rugged central North Island countryside, where they are looked after by two unusual characters, Boss and Pinkie. But, although they are kind, they have a no-nonsense approach to life and gradually help the boys to understand how their attitudes got them on the wrong side of the law.

William Taylor has seen at first hand the unhappiness crime can cause in small communities and in his unusual novel, *The Kidnap of Jessie Parker*, he takes a standard 'cops and robbers' situation, but then imagines the thoughts and feelings of both the 'bad' and the 'innocent' main characters. Jessie Parker is the thirteen-year-old daughter of a bank manager. She is kidnapped because she is the only witness to the armed robbery of her father's bank. Bound hand and foot, she spends a terrifying two days and nights at the mercy of an older boy, Spike. She realises that her only hope is to keep him talking and gradually, as she hears the story of his difficult childhood, she begins to feel sorry for him. But the book does not end happily with her escape — William Taylor follows the characters right through to the trial and shows there are no quick and easy answers to crime and that both Jessie and Spike are deeply affected by the incident.

His latest two books, *I Hate My Brother Maxwell Potter* and *The Porter Brothers*, both return to a more light-hearted mood and are about relationships between brothers — not always seen in the most flattering light.

William Taylor certainly never writes 'formula' books, and he is always exploring new ideas. Because his novels have been so successful overseas (they have been translated into German,

French, Dutch, Danish and Swedish, as well as being sold in other English-speaking countries), he recently gave up teaching for a while to write full-time. He aims to complete two novels a year, which is a heavy work load, but he says that everything is ready in his head before he puts anything down on paper, writing first in longhand, then typing on his old manual typewriter. He still does not like what he calls his 'posh electronic one'.

He really had intended to stop teaching and just enjoy being an author, but he missed the hurly-burly of school life and now he is back teaching again, because people are so important to him. He listens carefully to what they say and to the way they say it. His dialogue is always very true to life, and every character has a distinctive voice. It is one reason why his books have been so successful on television. He enjoys living in a small centre rather than in a big city: it is easier there to know people of all ages and from all walks of life. In William Taylor's books it is the characters who take command of the story and it is they whom we remember long after details of the plots have been forgotten.

BIBLIOGRAPHY

Books for children

Pack Up, Pick Up and Off. Price Milburn, Wellington, 1981.
My Summer of the Lions. Reed Methuen, Auckland, 1986.
Shooting Through. Reed Methuen, Auckland, 1986.
The Worst Soccer Team Ever. Reed Methuen, Auckland, 1987.
Break a Leg. Reed Methuen, Auckland, 1987.
Making Big Bucks. Reed Methuen, Auckland, 1987.
Possum Perkins. Ashton Scholastic, Auckland, 1987. Retitled *Paradise Lane.* Century Hutchinson, London, 1987.
The Kidnap of Jessie Parker. Heinemann Reed, Auckland, 1989.

I Hate My Brother Maxwell Potter. Heinemann Reed, Auckland, 1989.

The Porter Brothers. Collins, Auckland, 1990.

Agnes the Sheep. Ashton Scholastic, Auckland, 1990.

Books for adults

Fiction

Episode. Hale, London, 1970.

The Mask of the Clown. Hale, London, 1970.

The Plekhov Place. Hale, London, 1971.

Pieces in a Jigsaw. Hale, London, 1972.

The Persimmon Tree. Hale, London, 1972.

The Chrysalis. Hale, London, 1974.

Non-Fiction

The Third Day. Department of Education, Wellington, 1982.

Burnt Carrots Don't Have Legs. Dunmore Press, Palmerston North, 1976.

PHYL WARDELL

Born   Christchurch,
   21 October 1909. She has
   two grown-up children,
   and she lives in
   Christchurch.
Pets   She loves dogs,
   although she hasn't one at
   the moment. She has kept
   pigeons and bantams.
Favourite food   Chocolate!
Favourite pastimes   Reading,
   theatre-going, gardening, skipping and yoga.
Favourite authors   As a child: Ethel Turner's *Seven
   Little Australians*, Anna Sewell's *Black Beauty*,
   Conan Doyle's Sherlock Holmes books, R. M.
   Ballantyne's *Coral Island*. As an adult: Agatha
   Christie, Dorothy L. Sayers, P. D. James, Colette,
   P. G. Wodehouse, biographies and travel books.
Likes   Travel and exploring.
Dislikes   Rejection slips, although she thinks they
   have been useful in making her write and rewrite
   and learn the craft of being an author.
Profession   Before she married she was a secretary.

Phyl Wardell says, 'I didn't set out to write for children. I wanted
to write murder mysteries for adults. But a series of happenings
changed that. This is the way I came to write.

'My children were at school and I had some leisure. So I
took a course in journalism. Not with the idea of becoming
a writer of fiction, but I hoped it would teach me how to write

articles for magazines. The course gave me some confidence and the following year I wrote some articles and, to my surprise, actually sold a few. Every acceptance felt like winning a big lottery — though the pay was small. Two guineas per thousand words. I had a go at writing a book. It was an autobiography, which I later learned was the way most beginning authors start. By now I was keen. The next book was to be a light romance — except that a murder crept in. I enjoyed making up clues and suspense for that murder.

'I showed my books to an editor. He explained that they were not up to standard, though he praised the clues and suspense of the murder bits. This encouraged me to write a straight-out murder mystery. Nothing came of it, except that I was improving. I was planning another murder story, about an old miner prospecting for gold in a lonely, creepy bay, when the editor who had read my books asked me to write a serial for a children's magazine. It had to be full of action and adventure, with the episodes ending in cliff-hangers. He thought that because I had children I should know what children liked to read.

'Talk about not recognising opportunity when it struck! I had mixed feelings. Could I do it? Could I write a children's story? And what should I write about? Reluctantly I used the plot about the gold miner, altering it for children. Surprisingly, it was a lot of fun to do.'

The serial was called 'Gold at Kapai'. It was read on radio here and in Australia and was published as a book in Great Britain and New Zealand, and it was translated into German. The idea of using a gold miner in a story came from her own interest in the subject. Both her grandfathers had been gold miners. One had discovered the site of the Martha Mine in Thames and the other made such a big strike in Otago's famous Gabriel's Gully that he was able to set up a glassworks on the proceeds. But Phyl Wardell had never visited the old gold mines or learned how to pan for gold until she went on holiday with her husband and children to the West Coast.

She says, 'The glaciers, seals and relics of gold rushes thrilled us. The dark, lonely forests seemed scary to me. Even scarier was a visit to Gillespies Beach. At that time it had only one inhabitant — an old man who spent his days fossicking for gold. He showed us how to pan, and when some bright gold dust appeared, Bill, then fourteen, shouted with excitement, "Gold, Gold!" In that lonely place I thought how awful it would be if a villain were hiding among the trees and heard the cry of "Gold" and menaced this nice old man.'

It was another holiday that gave her the idea for her next book, *The Secret of the Lost Tribe.* They had taken a boat trip on beautiful Lake Te Anau and as they sailed along the western shores looking at the mountains and the bush, the ship's captain told them of a local legend. Many years ago, the Ngati Mamoe tribe had been chased into the bush by their enemies and had disappeared. He added, 'A lot of people think their descendants are still living there today.' He went on to describe how strange footprints had been found and mysterious camp fires had been sighted on the mountains.

Phyl Wardell's imagination was aroused. She remembered reading Conan Doyle's story 'The Lost World', and how for a long time afterwards she had been fascinated by that word 'lost'. Could there really be a lost tribe in that remote bush? Supposing there were, and a film company decided to find out? What would happen if they found the lost tribe? Would the tribe be happier to have cars and televisions — or would they be happier left to live as their ancestors had lived? To discover the answers to these questions you must read *The Secret of the Lost Tribe*!

The fiords also feature in her next book, *Passage to Dusky,* in which a father and his two children are on holiday in Dusky Sound and discover a cave containing stolen Maori artefacts . . .but other people are also after the treasure.

Phyl Wardell says she has often thought about writing a

science-fiction story, set in space. But she has always rejected the idea because 'the scenery would be so desolate'. Scenery is very important to her, especially the rivers, lakes and mountains of the South Island. She worries that they, and the creatures who inhabit them, may be threatened by human greed and carelessness. In a number of her books some aspect of New Zealand life is threatened and the main characters somehow manage to avert disaster.

The setting for *Hazard Island* is Stewart Island, where four teenagers on holiday uncover a ring of paua smugglers while they are investigating the mysterious disappearance of an Australian scuba diver. In *The Nelson Treasure* thirteen-year-old Ned is sure that the rare and possibly extinct huia is still alive in the North Island bush. But when he goes to find out, he discovers that the whole area is threatened by a property developer. In his battle to preserve the bush he is befriended by a strange man, Matt. There is something very mysterious about Matt, but the truth is not revealed until the very surprising ending.

Phyl Wardell's latest novel, *Beyond the Narrows*, shows what happens when nature is interfered with by an irresponsible scientist. His experiments to try to increase wool production go badly wrong and rumours of strange creatures in Fiordland have to be investigated...

It is better not to give away too many secrets about Phyl Wardell's books. There is some mystery in all of them, which the young heroes and heroines have to solve. They all have very tight plots. One thing leads to another in exciting episodes that keep the reader turning the pages. The books have to be carefully worked out before she begins writing. She has to know what happens at the end before she can start.

But first of all there is the research to be done. 'The fun part of writing is the research. During school holidays I would take my children on tenting trips to out-of-the-way places. We would talk to gold fossickers, deer stalkers, fishermen, launch skippers, a pilot, Maori elders, trampers and campers. Home again after these trips, I would visit the museum to check on bird life, the library to read early New Zealand history, go to botany and zoology lectures, and phone, write or call on people with special knowledge. Everyone was helpful. If this was work, it was a pleasure.

'The actual writing is a pleasure too. When it is going well. Even when it isn't, I still love it.'

BIBLIOGRAPHY

Gold at Kapai. Harrap, London, 1969.

The Secret of the Lost Tribe of Te Anau. Harrap, London, 1961. Retitled *The Secret of the Lost Tribe.* Hodder & Stoughton, Auckland, 1986.

Passage to Dusky. Parrish, London, 1967.

Hazard Island. Whitcoulls, Christchurch, 1976.

The Nelson Treasure. Hodder & Stoughton, Auckland, 1983.

Beyond the Narrows. Hodder & Stoughton, Auckland, 1985.

SOME MORE AUTHORS TO ENJOY

Question What do the following books have in common: *Alice in Wonderland*, *The Secret Garden*, *The Wind in the Willows*, *Winnie the Pooh*, *Peter Rabbit*, *Little Women* and *Anne of Green Gables*?

Answer All their authors are long since dead!

One of the best things about writing is that books live on long after their authors have died. Other countries of the world make sure that they keep their classics in print but in New Zealand sometimes very good books have disappeared because no one has republished them.

Here is a list of New Zealand authors now dead, but whose work is still to be found in libraries or even in bookshops, because they have all been reprinted within the last ten years. You will find that children do not change much and that a good story is a good story whether written today or fifty years ago.

Maurice Duggan 1922–74.

Maurice Duggan was a well-known writer for adults. He wrote only two children's books but one of them, *Falter Tom and the Water Boy*, is a particularly beautiful fantasy story about an old man who goes exploring beneath the sea, guided by a 'Water Boy'. First published in 1958, it won the New Zealand Library Association Esther Glen Award in 1959. It was reissued by Penguin Books in 1984.

Phillis Garrard

Phillis Garrard lived in New Zealand, in Taihape, for only two years, but she wrote a very entertaining and well-observed series of school stories about a New Zealand country school. She was writing in the 1930s, a time when school stories were extremely popular but mostly about boarding schools. Her books about a day school were unusual. The central character, Hilda, is a horse-riding heroine who is in Form I at the beginning of the series and has moved up to secondary school by the end. *Tales Out of School* was reissued in the Kotare series (Hodder & Stoughton) in 1984.

Esther Glen 1881–1940.

The New Zealand Library Association's major award for children's literature is the Esther Glen Award. It is named after a Christchurch journalist who worked first for the *Christchurch Sun* and later for *The Press*. She realised how few good, lively New Zealand books for children there were, and she started a special children's supplement in the *Christchurch Sun*, which published children's own writing. She also wrote *Six Little New Zealanders*, which was a New Zealand answer to Ethel Turner's *Seven Little Australians*. The six little New Zealanders are not so 'little' — they range in age from nine to nineteen — and when they go from Auckland to stay on their bachelor uncles' sheep station in Canterbury they manage to cause a considerable amount of chaos. *Six Little New Zealanders* and its sequel *Uncles Three at Kamahi* were first published in 1917 and 1926. They are funny, exciting and sometimes sad, but always memorable. They were reissued in the Kotare series (Hodder & Stoughton) in 1983 and 1985.

Edith Howes 1874–1954.

Edith Howes was a teacher at Wellington Girls' College and then in Gore. She was very interested in science and nature study and she wrote an enormous number of fantasy stories for young children, which have dated considerably. One novel she wrote for older readers, however, has become a New Zealand classic — *Silver Island*. It is the first New Zealand survival story and tells how a family of children are shipwrecked on a small island off Stewart Island and how they survive by living off the land. Then there is always the hope of finding treasure . . . *Silver Island* was first published in 1928 and was reissued in the Kotare series (Hodder & Stoughton) in 1984.

Isabel Maud Peacocke 1881–1973.

Isabel Maud Peacocke was an Auckland author who wrote no fewer than twenty-six full-length novels for children and seventeen for adults. She also wrote for radio, for the *New Zealand Herald* and for Whitcombe's Story Books. She was the first teacher at Dilworth School, where she read bedtime stories to the boys every night. She herself was brought up in the Auckland seaside suburbs of Cheltenham and Devonport and her book *The Cruise of the Crazy Jane* was New Zealand's first sailing story for children. It was published in 1932 and was reissued in the Kotare series (Hodder & Stoughton) in 1984.

Mona Tracy 1882–1959.

When Mona Tracy was only thirteen she persuaded the editor of the *Weekly News* to give her a job on the paper and later she trained as a reporter on the *New Zealand Herald*. She was one of New Zealand's first female journalists and later worked on the Christchurch *Press*. After she married in 1920 she stopped writing for newspapers but researched into New Zealand history and wrote a number of adult non-fiction books as well as giving numerous radio talks. Her best-known children's novel is *Rifle and Tomahawk*, which is an exciting story set at the time of Te Kooti. It shows how individuals can stay friends even if their families are on opposing sides in a war. *Rifle and Tomahawk* was first published in 1927 and was reissued in the *Kotare* series (Hodder & Stoughton) in 1983.

Joyce West 1908–85.

Both of Joyce West's parents were teachers and much of her childhood was spent in remote country schools. She started writing in her teens and had stories published in the *New Zealand Herald* and the *Weekly News*. She later wrote seven novels for adults and six for children. She was a very good horserider and her children's stories often feature gymkhanas or point-to-points. In her series beginning with *Drovers Road* she did for the North Island what Esther Glen had done for the Canterbury sheep stations, painting a vivid picture of country life. Her novel *The Year of the Shining Cuckoo* takes place in dairy-farming country in the far north. First published in 1963, it tells how Johnnie longed for a beautiful young filly, Golden Melody, but could never imagine that he would ever have enough money to buy her . . . *The Year of the Shining Cuckoo* was reissued in the Kotare series (Hodder & Stoughton) in 1985.

A suggestion for older readers

If you have enjoyed Ron Bacon's *Again the Bugles Blow*, go on to read about that same battle of Orakau in *The Greenstone Door*, a much longer novel by William Satchell, reprinted in a number of recent editions. If you liked the stories about early South Island settlers by Elsie Locke and Ruth Dallas, try reading two books written by Lady Barker, an early Canterbury settler. *Station Life in New Zealand* and *Station Amusements in New Zealand* have both been reissued in several editions in recent years.

SO YOU WANT TO BE A WRITER

Most children at school are told quite often to sit down and write something. Fortunately — or perhaps unfortunately — few adults are forced to do this. Certainly no one *has* to write fiction: authors are rather like mountaineers who climb mountains because they want to, and certainly not for the money.

You may have noticed that almost all the twenty-one writers in this book have something in common (apart from most of their being born between August and November). They all write and rewrite until they are satisfied. Joan de Hamel puts it neatly when she says, 'If it's true that the test of a vocation is the love of the drudgery it involves, then I must qualify as a writer with a vocation.' But how do they know when their writing has become 'good' enough? There is really only one answer to that and Margaret Mahy gives it when she says, 'To be a writer you must be a reader.' Almost all the authors in this book were bookworms when they were young. After all, we know that if young children never hear anyone speak they will never learn to talk. By the same token people who never read good books will find it hard to write well, because they have no standards by which to judge their work.

It has been said that writing is one part inspiration and three parts perspiration. Getting an idea is only the starting point: after that there's a great deal of work. However good a storyline it will only work if it is expressed in clear, interesting language and if it has a satisfying shape.

So what happens after a story has been written to the satisfaction of the author? A final draft is made, carefully typed in double spacing with good margins. It is then sent to a publisher. Why a publisher? Not many authors could afford to have several thousand copies of their own manuscript printed and bound, but a publisher may be prepared to do this if he or she thinks that the book will sell well. The person who makes this decision is an editor, who will read the manuscript and then either send it back to the author or decide to go ahead and publish it. This can be a risk. If the book proves to be a failure the publishers could be left with thousands of unsold copies and all the money spent on producing the book will have been wasted. Sometimes even if an editor likes a manuscript it may be turned down because it is not suitable for the market — that is to say that not many people would want to buy it.

But it can happen that one publishing firm rejects a book but another likes it. Two very famous books for children, Clive King's *Stig of the Dump* and Richard Adams's *Watership Down* had both been turned down by numerous publishers when their manuscripts arrived on the desk of Kaye Webb, a wonderful editor at Puffin Books. She immediately saw their worth and published them, and they became bestsellers.

The publishers take the responsibility of publishing a book and it is they who pay the author. Usually the author signs a contract with them agreeing to accept royalties, which means that they get a certain portion (often 10 per cent) of the price of every book sold. The disadvantage of this arrangement from the author's point of view is the length of time between writing a book and receiving any payment. If, for instance, a novel has taken a year to write, by the time it has found a publisher, been edited, typeset and printed, and been distributed to the bookshops, at least another year has passed by. Books do not necessarily sell straight away and most publishers only send out royalty cheques twice a year, so it will be another six months before the author receives any money — two-and-a-half years after first starting work on the book! Some publishers, however, will give an 'advance' on royalties, which means that the author gets some money before the book is published. Even then, 10 per cent of the price of each book is not much. Few authors are rich unless they are lucky enough to have written bestsellers.

Because there is such a long time between writing a book and receiving any income, most authors have to earn money in some other way. Barry Faville, for instance, is a full-time teacher. Even authors who devote their time entirely to writing may have to diversify — that is to say they may, like Maurice Gee and Margaret Mahy, write for television, or like both Margaret Mahy and Joy Cowley, write beginner readers for educational publishers. The money comes in sooner and in any case it is always interesting to try different ways of writing. Every form is a new challenge. Easy-reading books and television scripts are just as important to their readers and viewers as longer novels are to older children and adults.

Illustrations are very important in books for children — especially in picture books for younger children. Some authors, like Lynley Dodd, can do their own. Ronda Armitage works closely with her husband David. In general, though, it is the publisher who arranges an illustrator. Margaret Mahy has often been surprised by pictures given to her stories, especially in *The Ultra-Violet Catastrophe*. She had imagined a New Zealand weatherboard house with a manuka hedge but the English artist pictured it as a thatched cottage with a hawthorn hedge. Ron Bacon is one of the few writers who insists on knowing who will illustrate his work. He was the first children's writer to be adamant that Maori artists should be used for Maori stories.

If a book has done very well its publisher may take it to a wonderful book fair held every year in the Italian city of Bologna. Publishers from all over the world go there to look at books from other publishers, and if they like them, they buy the right to publish them in their own country. New Zealand books taken to Bologna may be seen by British, American, Danish, German, Dutch, French, Italian and Japanese publishers. If the rights to a book are sold, it is translated into the appropriate language, and off it goes to be sold in faraway countries. Margaret Mahy's books have been translated into fourteen different languages.

The book world is a fascinating one. It may be that some of you who are reading this now will enter it when you leave school. Perhaps you will go into publishing, work in a bookshop or, better still, become an illustrator or author. I hope that meeting these twenty-one writers will have given you a glimpse into the variety of people whose work has given New Zealand literature for children a firm base on which you — the authors of the future — will be able to build.